Lord Macaulay

Lays of Ancient Rome with Ivry and the Armada

Lord Macaulay

Lays of Ancient Rome with Ivry and the Armada

ISBN/EAN: 9783744764568

Printed in Europe, USA, Canada, Australia, Japan

Cover: Foto ©Andreas Hilbeck / pixelio.de

More available books at **www.hansebooks.com**

LAYS OF ANCIENT ROME

WITH

IVRY AND THE ARMADA

BY LORD MACAULAY

NEW EDITION

LONDON

LONGMANS, GREEN, AND CO.

1872

PREFACE.

THAT what is called the history of the Kings and early Consuls of Rome is to a great extent fabulous, few scholars have, since the time of Beaufort, ventured to deny. It is certain that, more than three hundred and sixty years after the date ordinarily assigned for the foundation of the city, the public records were, with scarcely an exception, destroyed by the Gauls. It is certain that the oldest annals of the commonwealth were compiled more than a century and a half after this destruction of the records. It is certain, therefore, that the great Latin writers of the Augustan age did not possess those materials, without which a trustworthy account of the infancy of the republic could not possibly be framed. Those writers own, indeed, that the chronicles to which they had access were filled with battles that were never fought, and Consuls that were never inaugurated; and we have abundant proof that, in these chronicles, events of the greatest importance, such as the issue of the war with Porsena, and the issue of the war with Brennus, were grossly mis-represented. Under these circumstances a wise man will look with great suspicion on the legend which has come down to us. He will perhaps be inclined to regard the princes who are said to have founded the civil and religious institutions of Rome, the son of Mars, and the husband of Egeria, as mere mythological personages, of the same class with Perseus and Ixion. As he draws nearer and nearer to the confines of authentic history, he will become less and less hard of belief. He will admit that the most important parts of the narrative have some foundation in truth. But he will distrust almost all the details, not only because they seldom rest on any solid evidence, but also because he will constantly detect in them, even when they are within the limits of physical possibility, that peculiar character, more easily understood than defined, which distinguishes the creations of the imagination from the realities of the world in which we live.

The early history of Rome is indeed far more poetical than anything else in Latin literature. The loves of the Vestal and the God of War, the cradle laid among the reeds of Tiber, the fig-tree, the she-wolf, the shepherd's cabin, the recognition, the fratricide, the rape of the Sabines, the death of Tarpeia, the fall of Hostus Hostilius, the struggle of Mettus Curtius through the marsh, the women rushing with torn raiment and dishevelled hair between their fathers and their husbands, the nightly meetings of Numa and the Nymph by the well in the sacred grove, the fight of the three Romans and the three Albans, the purchase of the Sibylline books, the crime of Tullia, the simulated madness of Brutus, the ambiguous reply of the Delphian oracle to the Tarquins, the wrongs of Lucretia, the heroic actions of Horatius Cocles, of Scævola, and of Clœlia, the battle of Regillus won by the aid of Castor and Pollux, the defence of Cremera, the touching story of Coriolanus, the still more touching story of Virginia, the wild legend about the draining of the Alban lake, the combat between Valerius Corvus and the gigantic Gaul, are among the many instances which will at once suggest themselves to every reader.

In the narrative of Livy, who was a man of fine imagination, these stories retain much of their genuine character. Nor could even the tasteless Dionysius distort and mutilate them into mere prose. The poetry shines, in spite of him, through the dreary pedantry of his eleven books. It is discernible in the most tedious and in the most superficial modern works on the early times of Rome. It enlivens the dulness of the Universal History, and gives a charm to the most meagre abridgements of Goldsmith.

Even in the age of Plutarch there were discerning men who rejected the popular account of the foundation of Rome, because that account appeared to them to have the air, not of a history, but of a romance or a drama. Plutarch, who was displeased at their incredulity, had nothing better to say in reply to their arguments than that chance sometimes turns poet, and produces trains of events not to be distinguished from the most elaborate plots which are constructed by art.* But though the existence of a poetical element in the early history of the Great City was detected so many years ago, the first critic who distinctly saw from what source that poetical element had been derived was James Perizonius, one of the most acute and learned antiquaries of the seventeenth century. His theory, which, in his own days, attracted little or no notice, was revived in the present generation by Niebuhr, a man who would have been the first writer of his time, if his talent for communicating truths had borne any proportion to his talent for investigating them. That theory has been adopted

---

* Ὕποπτον μὲν ἐνίοις ἐστὶ τὸ ϲραματικὸν καὶ πλασματῶϲες· οὐ ϲεῖ ϲὲ ἀπιστεῖν, τὴν τέχνην ὁρῶντας, οἵων ποιημάτων ϲημιουργός ἐστι.—Plut. Rom. viii. This remarkable passage has been more grossly misinterpreted than any other in the Greek language, where the sense was so obvious. The Latin version of Cruserius, the French version of Amyot, the old English version by several hands, and the later English version by Langhorne, are all equally destitute of every trace of the meaning of the original. None of the translators saw even that ποίημα is a poem. They all render it an event.

by several eminent scholars of our own country, particularly by the Bishop of St. David's, by Professor Malden, and by the lamented Arnold. It appears to be now generally received by men conversant with classical antiquity; and indeed it rests on such strong proofs, both internal and external, that it will not be easily subverted. A popular exposition of this theory, and of the evidence by which it is supported, may not be without interest even for readers who are unacquainted with the ancient languages.

The Latin literature which has come down to us is of later date than the commencement of the Second Punic War, and consists almost exclusively of works fashioned on Greek models. The Latin metres, heroic, elegiac, lyric, and dramatic, are of Greek origin. The best Latin epic poetry is the feeble echo of the Iliad and Odyssey. The best Latin eclogues are imitations of Theocritus. The plan of the most finished didactic poem in the Latin tongue was taken from Hesiod. The Latin tragedies are bad copies of the masterpieces of Sophocles and Euripides. The Latin comedies are free translations from Demophilus, Menander, and Apollodorus. The Latin philosophy was borrowed, without alteration, from the Portico and the Academy; and the great Latin orators constantly proposed to themselves as patterns the speeches of Demosthenes and Lysias.

But there was an earlier Latin literature, a literature truly Latin, which has wholly perished, which had, indeed, almost wholly perished long before those whom we are in the habit of regarding as the greatest Latin writers were born. That literature abounded with metrical romances, such as are found in every country where there is much curiosity and intelligence, but little reading and writing. All human beings, not utterly savage, long for some information about past times, and are delighted by narratives which present pictures to the eye of the mind. But it is only in very enlightened communities that books are readily accessible. Metrical composition, therefore, which, in a highly civilised nation, is a mere luxury, is, in nations imperfectly civilised, almost a necessary of life, and is valued less on account of the pleasure which it gives to the ear, than on account of the help which it gives to the memory. A man who can invent or embellish an interesting story, and put it into a form which others may easily retain in their recollection, will always be highly esteemed by a people eager for amusement and information, but destitute of libraries. Such is the origin of ballad-poetry, a species of composition which scarcely ever fails to spring up and flourish in every society, at a certain point in the progress towards refinement. Tacitus informs us that songs were the only memorials of the past which the ancient Germans possessed. We learn from Lucan and from Ammianus Marcellinus that the brave actions of the ancient Gauls were commemorated ·in the verses of Bards. During many ages, and through many revolutions, minstrelsy retained its influence over both the Teutonic and the Celtic race. The vengeance exacted by the spouse of Attila for the murder of Siegfried was celebrated in rhymes, of which Germany is still justly proud. The exploits of Athelstane were commemorated by the Anglo-Saxons, and those of Canute by the Danes, in rude poems, of which a few fragments have come down to us. The chants of the Welsh harpers preserved, through ages of darkness, a faint and doubtful memory of Arthur. In the Highlands of Scotland may still be gleaned some relics of the old songs about Cuthullin and Fingal. The long struggle of the Servians against the Ottoman power was recorded in lays full of martial spirit. We learn from Herrera that, when a Peruvian Inca died, men of skill were appointed to celebrate him in verses, which all the people learned by heart, and sang in public on days of festival. The feats of Kurroglou, the great free-booter of Turkistan, recounted in ballads composed by himself, are known in every village of Northern Persia. Captain Beechey heard the Bards of the Sandwich Islands recite the heroic achievements of Tamehameha, the most illustrious of their kings.

Mungo Park found in the heart of Africa a class of singing men, the only annalists of their rude tribes, and heard them tell the story of the victory which Damel, the negro prince of the Jaloffs, won over Abdulkader, the Mussulman tyrant of Foota Torra. This species of poetry attained a high degree of excellence among the Castilians, before they began to copy Tuscan patterns. It attained a still higher degree of excellence among the English and the Lowland Scotch, during the fourteenth, fifteenth, and sixteenth centuries. But it reached its full perfection in ancient Greece; for there can be no doubt that the great Homeric poems are generically ballads, though widely distinguished from all other ballads, and indeed from almost all other human compositions, by transcendent sublimity and beauty.

As it is agreeable to general experience that, at a certain stage in the progress of society, ballad-poetry should flourish, so is it also agreeable to general experience that, at a subsequent stage in the progress of society, ballad-poetry should be undervalued and neglected. Knowledge advances: manners change: great foreign models of composition are studied and imitated. The phraseology of the old minstrels becomes obsolete. Their versification, which, having received its laws only from the ear, abounds in irregularities, seems licentious and uncouth. Their simplicity appears beggarly when compared with the quaint forms and gaudy colouring of such artists as Cowley and Gongora. The ancient lays, unjustly despised by the learned and polite, linger for a time in the memory of the vulgar, and are at length too often irretrievably lost. We cannot wonder that the ballads of Rome should have altogether disappeared, when we remember how very narrowly, in spite of the invention of printing, those of our own country and those of Spain escaped the same fate. There is indeed little doubt that oblivion covers many English songs equal to any that were published by Bishop Percy, and many Spanish songs as good as the best of those which have been so happily translated by Mr. Lockhart. Eighty years ago England possessed only one tattered copy of Childe Waters and Sir Cauline, and Spain only one tattered copy of the noble poem of the Cid. The snuff of a candle, or a mischievous dog, might in a moment have deprived the world for ever of any of those fine compositions. Sir Walter Scott, who united to the fire of a great poet the minute curiosity and patient diligence of a great antiquary, was but just in time to save the precious relics of the Minstrelsy of the Border. In Germany, the lay of the Nibelungs had been long utterly forgotten, when, in the eighteenth century, it was, for the first time, printed from a manuscript in the old library of a noble family. In truth, the only people who, through their whole passage from simplicity to the highest civilisation, never for a moment ceased to love and admire their old ballads, were the Greeks.

That the early Romans should have had ballad-poetry, and that this poetry should have perished, is therefore not strange. It would, on the contrary, have been strange if these things had not come to pass; and we should be justified in pronouncing them highly probable, even if we had no direct evidence on the subject. But we have direct evidence of unquestionable authority.

Ennius, who flourished in the time of the Second Punic War, was regarded in the Augustan age as the father of Latin poetry. He was, in truth, the father of the second school of Latin poetry, the only school of which the works have descended to us. But from Ennius himself we learn that there were poets who stood to him in the same relation in which the author of the romance of Count Alarcos stood to Garcilaso, or the author of the 'Lytell Geste of Robyn Hode' to Lord Surrey. Ennius speaks of verses which the Fauns and the Bards were wont to chant in the old time, when none had yet studied the graces of speech, when none had yet climbed the peaks sacred to the Goddesses of Grecian song. 'Where,' Cicero mournfully asks, 'are those old verses now?'*

* 'Quid? Nostri veteres versus ubi sunt?

. . . . . . "Quos olim Fauni vatesque canebant.

Contemporary with Ennius was Quintus Fabius Pictor, the earliest of the Roman annalists. His account of the infancy and youth of Romulus and Remus has been preserved by Dionysius, and contains a very remarkable reference to the ancient Latin poetry. Fabius says that, in his time, his countrymen were still in the habit of singing ballads about the Twins. 'Even in the hut of Faustulus,'—so these old lays appear to have run,—'the children of Rhea and Mars were, in port and in spirit, not like unto swineherds or cowherds, but such that men might well guess fhem to be of the blood of Kings and Gods.' *

Cum neque Musarum scopulos quisquam superârat,
Nec dicti studiosus erat." '   *Brutus*, xviii.

The Muses, it should be observed, are Greek divinities. The Italian Goddesses of verse were the Camœnæ. At a later period, the appellations were used indiscriminately; but in the age of Ennius there was probably a distinction. In the epitaph of Nœvius, who was the representative of the old Italian school of poetry, the Camœnæ, not the Muses, are represented as grieving for the loss of their votary. The 'Musarum scopuli' are evidently the peaks of Parnassus.

Scaliger, in a note on Varro (*De Lingua Latina*, lib. vi.), suggests, with great ingenuity, that the Fauns, who were represented by the superstition of later ages as a race of monsters, half gods and half brutes, may really have been a class of men who exercised in Latium, at a very remote period, the same functions which belonged to the Magians in Persia and to the Bards in Gaul.

* Οἱ δὲ ἀνδρωθέντες γίνονται, κατά τε ἀξίωσιν μορφῆς καὶ φρονήματος ὄγκον, οὐ συοφορβοῖς καὶ βουκόλοις ἐοικότες, ἀλλ' οἵους ἄν τις ἀξιώσειε τοὺς ἐκ βασιλείου τε ὄντας γένους, καὶ ἀπὸ δαιμόνων

Cato the Censor, who also lived in the days of
the Second Punic War, mentioned this lost litera-

σπορᾶς γενέσθαι νομιζομένους, ὡς ἐν τοῖς πατρίοις ὕμνοις ὑπὸ
'Ρωμαίων ἔτι καὶ νῦν ᾄδεται.—*Dion. Hal.* i. 79. This passage
has sometimes been cited as if Dionysius had been speaking in
his own person, and had, Greek as he was, been so industrious
or so fortunate as to discover some valuable remains of that
early Latin poetry which the greatest Latin writers of his age
regretted as hopelessly lost. Such a supposition is highly
improbable; and indeed it seems clear from the context that
Dionysius, as Reiske and other editors evidently thought,
was merely quoting from Fabius Pictor. The whole passage
has the air of an extract from an ancient chronicle, and is
introduced by the words, Κόιντος μὲν Φάβιος, ὁ Πίκτωρ λεγόμενος,
τῇδε γράφει.

Another argument may be urged which seems to deserve
consideration. The author of the passage in question mentions
a thatched hut which, in his time, stood between the summit
of Mount Palatine and the Circus. This hut, he says, was built
by Romulus, and was constantly kept in repair at the public
charge, but never in any respect embellished. Now, in the
age of Dionysius there certainly was at Rome a thatched hut,
said to have been that of Romulus. But this hut, as we learn
from Vitruvius, stood, not near the Circus, but in the Capitol.
(*Vit.* ii. 1.) If, therefore, we understand Dionysius to speak in
his own person, we can reconcile his statement with that of
Vitruvius only by supposing that there were at Rome, in the
Augustan age, two thatched huts, both believed to have been
built by Romulus, and both carefully repaired and held in high
honour. The objections to such a supposition seem to be strong.
Neither Dionysius nor Vitruvius speaks of more than one such
hut. Dio Cassius informs us that twice, during the long administration of Augustus, the hut of Romulus caught fire.
(xlviii. 43, liv. 29.) Had there been two such huts, would he
not have told us of which he spoke? An English historian
would hardly give an account of a fire at Queen's College
without saying whether it was at Queen's College, Oxford, or
at Queen's College, Cambridge. Marcus Seneca, Macrobius,

ture in his lost work on the antiquities of his
country. Many ages, he said, before his time,
there were ballads in praise of illustrious men;
and these ballads it was the fashion for the guests
at banquets to sing in turn while the piper played.
'Would,' exclaims Cicero, 'that we still had the
old ballads of which Cato speaks!'*

and Conon, a Greek writer from whom Photius has made large
extracts, mention only one hut of Romulus, that in the Capitol.
(*M. Seneca, Contr.* i. 6.; *Macrobius, Sat.* i. 15.; *Photius, Bibl.* 186.)
Ovid, Livy, Petronius, Valerius Maximus, Lucius Seneca, and
St. Jerome, mention only one hut of Romulus, without speci-
fying the site. (*Ovid. Fasti,* iii. 183.; *Liv.* v. 53.; *Petronius,
Fragm.; Val. Max.* iv. 4.; *L. Seneca, Consolatio ad Helviam;
D. Hieron. ad Paulinianum de Didymo.*)

The whole difficulty is removed, if we suppose that Dionysius was merely quoting Fabius Pictor. Nothing is more
probable than that the cabin, which in the time of Fabius
stood near the Circus, might, long before the age of Augustus,
have been transported to the Capitol, as the place fittest, by
reason both of its safety and of its sanctity, to contain so precious a relic.

The language of Plutarch confirms this hypothesis. He
describes, with great precision, the spot where Romulus dwelt,
on the slope of Mount Palatine leading to the Circus; but he
says not a word implying that the dwelling was still to be seen
there. Indeed, his expressions imply that it was no longer
there. The evidence of Solinus is still more to the point. He,
like Plutarch, describes the spot where Romulus had resided,
and says expressly that the hut had been there, but that in his
time it was there no longer. The site, it is certain, was well
remembered: and probably retained its old name, as Charing
Cross and the Haymarket have done. This is probably the
explanation of the words 'casa Romuli,' in Victor's description of the Tenth Region of Rome, under Valentinian.

* Cicero refers twice to this important passage in Cato's

Valerius Maximus gives us exactly similar information, without mentioning his authority, and observes that the ancient Roman ballads were probably of more benefit to the young than all the lectures of the Athenian schools, and that to the influence of the national poetry were to be ascribed the virtues of such men as Camillus and Fabricius.*

Varro, whose authority on all questions connected with the antiquities of his country is entitled to the greatest respect, tells us that at banquets it was once the fashion for boys to sing, sometimes with and sometimes without instrumental music, ancient ballads in praise of men of former times. These young performers, he observes, were of unblemished character, a circumstance which he probably mentioned because, among the Greeks, and indeed in his time among the Romans

Antiquities :—'Gravissimus auctor in Originibus dixit Cato, morem apud majores hunc epularum fuisse, ut deinceps, qui accubarent, canerent ad tibiam clarorum virorum laudes atque virtutes. Ex quo perspicuum est, et cantus tum fuisse rescriptos vocum sonis, et carmina.'—*Tusc. Quæst.* iv. 2. Again : 'Utinam exstarent illa carmina, quæ, multis sæculis ante suam ætatem, in epulis esse cantitata a singulis convivis de clarorum virorum laudibus, in Originibus scriptum reliquit Cato.'—*Brutus*, xix.

* 'Majores natu in conviviis ad tibias egregia superiorum opera carmine comprehensa pangebant, quo ad ea imitanda juventutem alacriorem redderent. . . . Quas Athenas, quam scholam, quæ alienigena studia huic domesticæ disciplinæ prætulerim? Inde oriebantur Camilli, Scipiones, Fabricii, Marcelli, Fabii.'—*Val. Max.* ii. 1.

also, the morals of singing boys were in no high repute.*

The testimony of Horace, though given incidentally, confirms the statements of Cato, Valerius Maximus, and Varro. The poet predicts that, under the peaceful administration of Augustus, the Romans will, over their full goblets, sing to the pipe, after the fashion of their fathers, the deeds of brave captains, and the ancient legends touching the origin of the city.†

The proposition, then, that Rome had ballad-poetry is not merely in itself highly probable, but is fully proved by direct evidence of the greatest weight.

This proposition being established, it becomes easy to understand why the early history of the city is unlike almost everything else in Latin literature, native where almost everything else is borrowed, imaginative where almost everything

* 'In conviviis pueri modesti ut cantarent carmina antiqua, in quibus laudes erant majorum, et assa voce, et cum tibicine.' Nonius, *Assa voce pro sola.*

  † 'Nosque et profestis lucibus et sacris,
   Inter jocosi munera Liberi,
    Cum prole matronisque nostris,
    Rite Deos prius apprecati,
   Virtute functos, more patrum, duces,
   Lydis remixto carmine tibiis,
    Trojamque, et Anchisen, et almæ
    Progeniem Veneris canemus.'
         Carm. iv. 15.

else is prosaic. We can scarcely hesitate to pronounce that the magnificent, pathetic, and truly national legends, which present so striking a contrast to all that surrounds them, are broken and defaced fragments of that early poetry which, even in the age of Cato the Censor, had become antiquated, and of which Tully had never heard a line.

That this poetry should have been suffered to perish will not appear strange when we consider how complete was the triumph of the Greek genius over the public mind of Italy. It is probable that, at an early period, Homer and Herodotus furnished some hints to the Latin minstrels:* but it was not till after the war with Pyrrhus that the poetry of Rome began to put off its old Ausonian character. The transformation was soon consummated. The conquered, says Horace, led captive the conquerors. It was precisely at the time at which the Roman people rose to unrivalled political ascendency that they stooped to pass under the intellectual yoke. It was precisely at the time at which the sceptre departed from Greece that the empire of her language and of her arts became universal and despotic. The revolution indeed was not effected without a struggle. Nævius seems to have been the last of the ancient line of poets. Ennius was the

* See the Preface to the Lay of the Battle of Regillus.

founder of a new dynasty. Nævius celebrated
the First Punic War in Saturnian verse, the old
national verse of Italy.* Ennius sang the Second

* Cicero speaks highly in more than one place of this poem
of Nævius; Ennius sneered at it, and stole from it.

As to the Saturnian measure, see Hermann's *Elementa
Doctrinæ Metricæ*, iii. 9.

The Saturnian line, according to the grammarians, consisted
of two parts. The first was a catalectic dimeter iambic; the
second was composed of three trochees. But the licence taken
by the early Latin poets seems to have been almost boundless.
The most perfect Saturnian line which has been preserved was
the work, not of a professional artist, but of an amateur:

'Dabunt malum Metelli Nævio poetæ.'

There has been much difference of opinion among learned
men respecting the history of this measure. That it is the
same with a Greek measure used by Archilochus is in-
disputable. (*Bentley, Phalaris*, xi.) But in spite of the authority of Terentianus Maurus, and of the still higher authority
of Bentley, we may venture to doubt whether the coincidence
was not fortuitous. We constantly find the same rude and
simple numbers in different countries, under circumstances
which make it impossible to suspect that there has been
imitation on either side. Bishop Heber heard the children of a
village in Bengal singing 'Radha, Radha,' to the tune of 'My
boy Billy.' Neither the Castilian nor the German minstrels of
the middle ages owed anything to Paros or to ancient Rome.
Yet both the poem of the Cid and the poem of the Nibelungs
contain many Saturnian verses; as,—

'Estas nuevas á mio Cid eran venidas.'

'Á mi lo dicen; á ti dan las orejadas.'

'Man möhte michel wunder von Sifride sagen.'

'Wa ich den Künic vinde daz sol man mir sagen.'

Indeed, there cannot be a more perfect Saturnian line than one
which is sung in every English nursery—

'The queen was in her parlour eating bread and honey;'

Punic War in numbers borrowed from the Iliad.
The elder poet, in the epitaph which he wrote

yet the author of this line, we may be assured, borrowed
nothing from either Nævius or Archilochus.

On the other hand, it is by no means improbable that, two
or three hundred years before the time of Ennius, some Latin
minstrel may have visited Sybaris or Crotona, may have heard
some verses of Archilochus sung, may have been pleased with
the metre, and may have introduced it at Rome. Thus much
is certain, that the Saturnian measure, if not a native of Italy,
was at least so early and so completely naturalised there that
its foreign origin was forgotten.

Bentley says indeed that the Saturnian measure was first
brought from Greece into Italy by Nævius. But this is
merely *obiter dictum*, to use a phrase common in our courts of
law, and would not have been deliberately maintained by that
incomparable critic, whose memory is held in reverence by all
lovers of learning. The arguments which might be brought
against Bentley's assertion—for it is mere assertion, supported
by no evidence—are innumerable. A few will suffice.

1. Bentley's assertion is opposed to the testimony of Ennius.
Ennius sneered at Nævius for writing on the First Punic War
in verses such as the old Italian Bards used before Greek literature had been studied. Now the poem of Nævius was in
Saturnian verse. Is it possible that Ennius could have used
such expressions, if the Saturnian verse had been just imported
from Greece for the first time?

2. Bentley's assertion is opposed to the testimony of Horace.
'When Greece,' says Horace, 'introduced her arts into our un-
civilised country, those rugged Saturnian numbers passed away.'
Would Horace have said this, if the Saturnian numbers had
been imported from Greece just before the hexameter?

3. Bentley's assertion is opposed to the testimony of Festus
and of Aurelius Victor, both of whom positively say that the
most ancient prophecies attributed to the Fauns were in Saturnian verse.

4. Bentley's assertion is opposed to the testimony of Teren-

for himself, and which is a fine specimen of the
early Roman diction and versification, plaintively
boasted that the Latin language had died with
him.* Thus what to Horace appeared to be the
first faint dawn of Roman literature, appeared to
Nœvius to be its hopeless setting. In truth, one
literature was setting, and another dawning.

The victory of the foreign taste was decisive :
and indeed we can hardly blame the Romans for
turning away with contempt from the rude lays
which had delighted their fathers, and giving
their whole admiration to the immortal productions of Greece. The national romances, neglected
by the great and the refined whose education had
been finished at Rhodes or Athens, continued, it
may be supposed, during some generations, to

tianus Maurus, to whom he has himself appealed. Terentianus
Maurus does indeed say that the Saturnian measure, though
believed by the Romans from a very early period ('credidit
vetustas') to be of Italian invention, was really borrowed from
the Greeks. But Terentianus Maurus does not say that it was
first borrowed by Nœvius. Nay, the expressions used by Terentianus Maurus clearly imply the contrary: for how could
the Romans have believed, from a very early period, that this
measure was the indigenous production of Latium, if it was
really brought over from Greece in an age of intelligence and
liberal curiosity, in the age which gave birth to Ennius, Plautus,
Cato the Censor, and other distinguished writers? If Bentley's
assertion were correct, there could have been no more doubt at
Rome about the Greek origin of the Saturnian measure than
about the Greek origin of hexameters or Sapphics.

* Aulus Gellius, Noctes Atticæ, i. 24.

delight the vulgar. While Virgil, in hexameters of exquisite modulation, described the sports of rustics, those rustics were still singing their wild Saturnian ballads.* It is not improbable that, at the time when Cicero lamented the irreparable loss of the poems mentioned by Cato, a search among the nooks of the Apennines, as active as the search which Sir Walter Scott made among the descendants of the mosstroopers of Liddesdale, might have brought to light many fine remains of ancient minstrelsy. No such search was made. The Latin ballads perished for ever. Yet discerning critics have thought that they could still perceive in the early history of Rome numerous fragments of this lost poetry, as the traveller on classic ground sometimes finds, built into the heavy wall of a fort or convent, a pillar rich with acanthus leaves, or a frieze where the Amazons and Bacchanals seem to live. The theatres and temples of the Greek and the Roman were degraded into the quarries of the Turk and the Goth. Even so did the ancient Saturnian poetry become the quarry in which a crowd of orators and annalists found the materials for their prose.

It is not difficult to trace the process by which the old songs were transmuted into the form which they now wear. Funeral panegyric and chronicle appear to have been the intermediate links which

* See Servius, in Georg. ii. 385.

connected the lost ballads with the histories now extant. From a very early period it was the usage that an oration should be pronounced over the remains of a noble Roman. The orator, as we learn from Polybius, was expected, on such an occasion, to recapitulate all the services which the ancestors of the deceased had, from the earliest time, rendered to the commonwealth. There can be little doubt that the speaker on whom this duty was imposed would make use of all the stories suited to his purpose which were to be found in the popular lays. There can be as little doubt that the family of an eminent man would preserve a copy of the speech which had been pronounced over his corpse. The compilers of the early chronicles would have recourse to these speeches; and the great historians of a later period would have recourse to the chronicles.

It may be worth while to select a particular story, and to trace its probable progress through these stages. The description of the migration of the Fabian house to Cremera is one of the finest of the many fine passages which lie thick in the earlier books of Livy. The Consul, clad in his military garb, stands in the vestibule of his house, marshalling his clan, three hundred and six fighting men, all of the same proud patrician blood, all worthy to be attended by the fasces, and to command the legions. A sad and anxious

retinue of friends accompanies the adventurers
through the streets; but the voice of lamentation
is drowned by the shouts of admiring thousands.
As the procession passes the Capitol, prayers and
vows are poured forth, but in vain. The devoted
band, leaving Janus on the right, marches to its
doom through the Gate of Evil Luck. After achiev-
ing high deeds of valour against overwhelming
numbers, all perish save one child, the stock from
which the great Fabian race was destined again to
spring for the safety and glory of the commonwealth. That this fine romance, the details of
which are so full of poetical truth, and so utterly
destitute of all show of historical truth, came
originally from some lay which had often been
sung with great applause at banquets, is in the
highest degree probable. Nor is it difficult to
imagine a mode in which the transmission might
have taken place. The celebrated Quintus Fabius
Maximus, who died about twenty years before the
First Punic War, and more than forty years before
Ennius was born, is said to have been interred
with extraordinary pomp. In the eulogy pronounced over his body all the great exploits of
his ancestors were doubtless recounted and exaggerated. If there were then extant songs which
gave a vivid and touching description of an event,
the saddest and the most glorious in the long
history of the Fabian house, nothing could be

more natural than that the panegyrist should borrow from such songs their finest touches, in order to adorn his speech. A few generations later the songs would perhaps be forgotten, or remembered only by shepherds and vine-dressers. But the speech would certainly be preserved in the archives of the Fabian nobles. Fabius Pictor would be well acquainted with a document so interesting to his personal feelings, and would insert large extracts from it in his rude chronicle. That chronicle, as we know, was the oldest to which Livy had access. Livy would at a glance distinguish the bold strokes of the forgotten poet from the dull and feeble narrative by which they were surrounded, would retouch them with a delicate and powerful pencil, and would make them immortal.

That this might happen at Rome can scarcely be doubted; for something very like this has happened in several countries, and, among others, in our own. Perhaps the theory of Perizonius cannot be better illustrated than by showing that what he supposes to have taken place in ancient times has, beyond all doubt, taken place in modern times.

'History,' says Hume with the utmost gravity, 'has preserved some instances of Edgar's amours, from which, as from a specimen, we may form a conjecture of the rest.' He then tells very agree-

ably the stories of Elfleda and Elfrida, two stories
which have a most suspicious air of romance, and
which, indeed, greatly resemble, in their general
character, some of the legends of early Rome. He
cites, as his authority for these two tales, the
chronicle of William of Malmesbury, who lived
in the time of King Stephen. The great majority
of readers suppose that the device by which Elfrida
was substituted for her young mistress, the artifice
by which Athelwold obtained the hand of Elfrida,
the detection of that artifice, the hunting party,
and the vengeance of the amorous king, are
things about which there is no more doubt than
about the execution of Anne Boleyn, or the
slitting of Sir John Coventry's nose. But when
we turn to William of Malmesbury, we find that
Hume, in his eagerness to relate these pleasant
fables, has overlooked one very important circumstance. William does indeed tell both the stories ;
but he gives us distinct notice that he does not
warrant their truth, and that they rest on no
better authority than that of ballads.*

Such is the way in which these two well-known
tales have been handed down. They originally
appeared in a poetical form. They found their

---

* 'Infamias quas post dicam magis resperserunt cantilenæ.'
Edgar appears to have been most mercilessly treated in the
Anglo-Saxon ballads. He was the favourite of the monks;
and the monks and the minstrels were at deadly feud.

way from ballads into an old chronicle. The ballads perished; the chronicle remained. A great historian, some centuries after the ballads had been altogether forgotten, consulted the chronicle. He was struck by the lively colouring of these ancient fictions: he transferred them to his pages; and thus we find inserted, as unquestionable facts, in a narrative which is likely to last as long as the English tongue, the inventions of some minstrel whose works were probably never committed to writing, whose name is buried in oblivion, and whose dialect has become obsolete. It must, then, be admitted to be possible, or rather highly probable, that the stories of Romulus and Remus, and of the Horatii and Curiatii, may have had a similar origin.

Castilian literature will furnish us with another parallel case. Mariana, the classical historian of Spain, tells the story of the ill-starred marriage which the King Don Alonso brought about between the heirs of Carrion and the two daughters of the Cid. The Cid bestowed a princely dower on his sons-in-law. But the young men were base and proud, cowardly and cruel. They were tried in danger, and found wanting. They fled before the Moors, and once, when a lion broke out of his den, they ran and crouched in an unseemly hiding-place. They knew that they were despised, and took counsel how they might be avenged. They parted from their father-in-law with many signs of love, and set forth on a journey with Doña Elvira and Doña Sol. In a solitary place the bridegrooms seized their brides, stripped them, scourged them, and departed, leaving them for dead. But one of the house of Bivar, suspecting foul play, had followed the travellers in disguise. The ladies were brought back safe to the house of their father. Complaint was made to the king. It was adjudged by the Cortes that the dower given by the Cid should be returned, and that the heirs of Carrion together with one of their kindred should do battle against three knights of the party of the Cid. The guilty youths would have declined the combat; but all their shifts were vain. They were vanquished in the lists, and for ever disgraced, while their injured wives were sought in marriage by great princes.*

Some Spanish writers have laboured to show, by an examination of dates and circumstances, that this story is untrue. Such confutation was surely not needed; for the narrative is on the face of it a romance. How it found its way into Mariana's history is quite clear. He acknowledges his obligations to the ancient chronicles; and had doubtless before him the 'Cronica del famoso Cavallero Cid Ruy Diez Campeador,' which

* Mariana, lib. x. cap. 4.

had been printed as early as the year 1552. He little suspected that all the most striking passages in this chronicle were copied from a poem of the twelfth century, a poem of which the language and versification had long been obsolete, but which glowed with no common portion of the fire of the Iliad. Yet such was the fact. More than a century and a half after the death of Mariana, this venerable ballad, of which one imperfect copy on parchment, four hundred years old, had been preserved at Bivar, was for the first time printed. Then it was found that every interesting circumstance of the story of the heirs of Carrion was derived by the eloquent Jesuit from a song of which he had never heard, and which was composed by a minstrel whose very name had long been forgotten.*

Such, or nearly such, appears to have been the process by which the lost ballad-poetry of Rome was transformed into history. To reverse that process, to transform some portions of early Roman history back into the poetry out of which they were made, is the object of this work.

In the following poems the author speaks, not in his own person, but in the persons of ancient

* See the account which Sanchez gives of the Bivar manuscript in the first volume of the *Coleccion de Poesias Castellanas anteriores al Siglo XV*. Part of the story of the lords of Carrion, in the poem of the Cid, has been translated by Mr. Frere in a manner above all praise.

minstrels who know only what a Roman citizen, born three or four hundred years before the Christian æra, may be supposed to have known, and who are in nowise above the passions and prejudices of their age and nation. To these imaginary poets must be ascribed some blunders which are so obvious that it is unnecessary to point them out. The real blunder would have been to represent these old poets as deeply versed in general history, and studious of chronological accuracy. To them must also be attributed the illiberal sneers at the Greeks, the furious party-spirit, the contempt for the arts of peace, the love of war for its own sake, the ungenerous exultation over the vanquished, which the reader will sometimes observe. To portray a Roman of the age of Camillus or Curius as superior to national antipathies, as mourning over the devastation and slaughter by which empire and triumphs were to be won, as looking on human suffering with the sympathy of Howard, or as treating conquered enemies with the delicacy of the Black Prince, would be to violate all dramatic propriety. The old Romans had some great virtues, fortitude, temperance, veracity, spirit to resist oppression, respect for legitimate authority, fidelity in the observing of contracts, disinterestedness, ardent patriotism ; but Christian charity and chivalrous generosity were alike unknown to them.

It would have been obviously improper to mimic
the manner of any particular age or country.
Something has been borrowed, however, from our
own old ballads, and more from Sir Walter Scott,
the great restorer of our ballad-poetry. To the
Iliad still greater obligations are due; and those
obligations have been contracted with the less
hesitation, because there is reason to believe that
some of the old Latin minstrels really had recourse to that inexhaustible store of poetical
images.

It would have been easy to swell this little
volume to a very considerable bulk, by append-
ing notes filled with quotations; but to a learned
reader such notes are not necessary; for an unlearned reader they would have little interest;
and the judgment passed both by the learned and
by the unlearned on a work of the imagination
will always depend much more on the general
character and spirit of such a work than on
minute details.

HORATIUS.

C

HORATIUS.

THERE can be little doubt that among those parts of early Roman history which had a poetical origin was the legend of Horatius Cocles. We have several versions of the story, and these versions differ from each other in points of no small importance. Polybius, there is reason to believe, heard the tale recited over the remains of some Consul or Prætor descended from the old Horatian patricians; for he introduces it as a specimen of the narratives with which the Romans were in the habit of embellishing their funeral oratory. It is remarkable that, according to him, Horatius defended the bridge alone, and perished in the waters. According to the chronicles which Livy and Dionysius followed, Horatius had two companions, swam safe to shore, and was loaded with honours and rewards.

These discrepancies are easily explained. Our own literature, indeed, will furnish an exact parallel to what may have taken place at Rome. It is highly probable that the memory of the war of Porsena was preserved by compositions much resembling the two ballads which stand first in the *Relics of Ancient English Poetry*. In both those ballads the English, commanded by the Percy, fight with the Scots, commanded by the Douglas. In one of the ballads the Douglas is killed by a nameless English archer, and the Percy by a Scottish spearman : in the other, the Percy slays the Douglas in single combat, and is himself made prisoner. In the former, Sir Hugh Montgomery is shot through the heart by a Northumbrian bowman : in the latter he is taken, and exchanged for the Percy. Yet both the ballads relate to the same event, and that an event which probably took place within the memory of persons who were alive when both the ballads were made. One of the minstrels says :

'Old men that knowen the grounde well yenoughe
Call it the battell of Otterburn :
At Otterburn began this spurne
Upon a monnyn day.
Ther was the dongghte Doglas slean :
The Perse never went away.'

The other poet sums up the event in the following lines :

'Thys fraye bygan at Otterborne
Bytwene the nyghte and the day :
Ther the Dowglas lost hys lyfe,
And the Percy was lede away.'

It is by no means unlikely that there were two old Roman lays about the defence of the bridge; and that, while the story which Livy has transmitted to us was preferred by the multitude, the other, which ascribed the whole glory to Horatius alone, may have been the favourite with the Horatian house.

The following ballad is supposed to have been made about a hundred and twenty years after the war which it celebrates, and just before the taking of Rome by the Gauls. The author seems to have been an honest citizen, proud of the military glory of his country, sick of the disputes of factions, and much given to pining after good old times which had never really existed. The allusion, however, to the partial manner in which the public lands were allotted could proceed only from a plebeian; and the allusion to the fraudulent sale of spoils marks the date of the poem, and shows that the poet shared in the general discontent with which the proceedings of Camillus, after the taking of Veii, were regarded.

The penultimate syllable of the name Porsena has been shortened in spite of the authority of Niebuhr, who pronounces, without assigning any ground for his opinion, that Martial was guilty of a decided blunder in the line,

'Hanc spectare manum Porsena non potuit.'

It is not easy to understand how any modern

scholar, whatever his attainments may be,—and
those of Niebuhr were undoubtedly immense,—
can venture to pronounce that Martial did not
know the quantity of a word which he must have
uttered and heard uttered a hundred times before
he left school.   Niebuhr seems also to have forgotten that Martial has fellow-culprits to keep
him in countenance.   Horace has committed the
same decided blunder; for he gives us, as a pure
iambic line,

> 'Minacis aut Etrusca Porsenæ manus.'

Silius Italicus has repeatedly offended in the same
way, as when he says,

> 'Cernitur effugiens ardentem Porsena dextram:'

and again,

> 'Clusinum vulgus, cum, Porsena magne, jubebas.'

A modern writer may be content to err in such
company.

Niebuhr's supposition that each of the three
defenders of the bridge was the representative of
one of the three patrician tribes is both ingenious
and probable, and has been adopted in the following poem.

HORATIUS.

A LAY MADE ABOUT THE YEAR OF THE CITY
CCCLX.

———◆◇◆———

I.

Lars Porsena of Clusium
　By the Nine Gods he swore
That the great house of Tarquin
　Should suffer wrong no more.
By the Nine Gods he swore it,
　And named a trysting day,
And bade his messengers ride forth,
East and west and south and north,
　To summon his array.

II.

East and west and south and north
　The messengers ride fast,
And tower and town and cottage
　Have heard the trumpet's blast.
Shame on the false Etruscan
　Who lingers in his home,
When Porsena of Clusium
　Is on the march for Rome.

III.

The horsemen and the footmen
    Are pouring in amain
From many a stately market-place;
    From many a fruitful plain;
From many a lonely hamlet,
    Which, hid by beech and pine,
Like an eagle's nest, hangs on the crest
    Of purple Apennine;

IV.

From lordly Volaterræ,
    Where scowls the far-famed hold
Piled by the hands of giants
    For godlike kings of old;
From seagirt Populonia,
    Whose sentinels descry
Sardinia's snowy mountain-tops
    Fringing the southern sky;

V.

From the proud mart of Pisæ,
    Queen of the western waves,
Where ride Massilia's triremes
    Heavy with fair-haired slaves;
From where sweet Clanis wanders
    Through corn and vines and flowers;
From where Cortona lifts to heaven
    Her diadem of towers.

VI.

Tall are the oaks whose acorns
  Drop in dark Auser's rill;
Fat are the stags that champ the boughs
  Of the Ciminian hill;
Beyond all streams Clitumnus
  Is to the herdsman dear;
Best of all pools the fowler loves
  The great Volsinian mere.

VII.

But now no stroke of woodman
  Is heard by Auser's rill;
No hunter tracks the stag's green path
  Up the Ciminian hill;
Unwatched along Clitumnus
  Grazes the milk-white steer;
Unharmed the water fowl may dip
  In the Volsinian mere.

VIII.

The harvests of Arretium,
  This year, old men shall reap,
This year, young boys in Umbro
  Shall plunge the struggling sheep;
And in the vats of Luna,
  This year, the must shall foam
Round the white feet of laughing girls
  Whose sires have marched to Rome.

IX.

There be thirty chosen prophets,
　The wisest of the land,
Who alway by Lars Porsena
　Both morn and evening stand:
Evening and morn the Thirty
　Have turned the verses o'er,
Traced from the right on linen white
　By mighty seers of yore.

X.

And with one voice the Thirty
　Have their glad answer given:
' Go forth, go forth, Lars Porsena;
　Go forth, beloved of Heaven;
Go, and return in glory
　To Clusium's royal dome;
And hang round Nurscia's altars
　The golden shields of Rome.'

XI.

And now hath every city
　Sent up her tale of men;
The foot are fourscore thousand,
　The horse are thousands ten:
Before the gates of Sutrium
　Is met the great array.
A proud man was Lars Porsena
　' Upon the trysting day.

XII.

For all the Etruscan armies
   Were ranged beneath his eye,
And many a banished Roman,
   And many a stout ally;
And with a mighty following
   To join the muster came
The Tusculan Mamilius,
   Prince of the Latian name.

XIII.

But by the yellow Tiber
   Was tumult and affright:
From all the spacious champaign
   To Rome men took their flight.
A mile around the city,
   The throng stopped up the ways;
A fearful sight it was to see
   Through two long nights and days.

XIV.

For aged folks on crutches,
   And women great with child,
And mothers sobbing over babes
   That clung to them and smiled.
And sick men borne in litters
   High on the necks of slaves,
And troops of sun-burned husbandmen
   With reaping-hooks and staves,

XV.

And droves of mules and asses
  Laden with skins of wine,
And endless flocks of goats and sheep,
  And endless herds of kine,
And endless trains of waggons
  That creaked beneath the weight
Of corn-sacks and of household goods,
  Choked every roaring gate.

XVI.

Now, from the rock Tarpeian,
  Could the wan burghers spy
The line of blazing villages
  Red in the midnight sky.
The Fathers of the City,
  They sat all night and day,
For every hour some horseman came
  With tidings of dismay.

XVII.

To eastward and to westward
  Have spread the Tuscan bands;
Nor house, nor fence, nor dovecote
  In Crustumerium stands.
Verbenna down to Ostia
  Hath wasted all the plain;
Astur hath stormed Janiculum,
  And the stout guards are slain.

XVIII.

I wis, in all the Senate,
　　There was no heart so bold,
But sore it ached, and fast it beat,
　　When that ill news was told.
Forthwith up rose the Consul,
　　Up rose the Fathers all;
In haste they girded up their gowns,
　　And hied them to the wall.

XIX.

They held a council standing
　　Before the River-Gate;
Short time was there, ye well may guess,
　　For musing or debate.
Out spake the Consul roundly:
　　'The bridge must straight go down;
For, since Janiculum is lost,
　　Nought else can save the town.'

XX.

Just then a scout came flying,
　　All wild with haste and fear:
'To arms! to arms! Sir Consul:
　　Lars Porsena is here.'
On the low hills to westward
　　The Consul fixed his eye,
And saw the swarthy storm of dust
　　Rise fast along the sky.

XXI.

And nearer fast and nearer
  Doth the red whirlwind come ;
And louder still and still more loud,
From underneath that rolling cloud,
Is heard the trumpet's war-note proud,
  The trampling, and the hum.
And plainly and more plainly
  Now through the gloom appears,
Far to left and far to right,
In broken gleams of dark-blue light,
The long array of helmets bright,
  The long array of spears.

XXII.

And plainly and more plainly,
  Above that glimmering line,
Now might ye see the banners
  Of twelve fair cities shine ;
But the banner of proud Clusium
  Was highest of them all,
The terror of the Umbrian,
  The terror of the Gaul.

XXIII.

And plainly and more plainly
  Now might the burghers know,
By port and vest, by horse and crest,
  Each warlike Lucumo.

There Cilnius of Arretium
  On his fleet roan was seen;
And Astur of the four-fold shield,
Girt with the brand none else may wield,
Tolumnius with the belt of gold,
And dark Verbenna from the hold
  By reedy Thrasymene.

XXIV.

Fast by the royal standard,
  O'erlooking all the war,
Lars Porsena of Clusium
  Sat in his ivory car.
By the right wheel rode Mamilius,
  Prince of the Latian name;
And by the left false Sextus,
  That wrought the deed of shame.

XXV.

But when the face of Sextus
  Was seen among the foes,
A yell that rent the firmament
  From all the town arose.
On the house-tops was no woman
  But spat towards him and hissed,
No child but screamed out curses,
  And shook its little fist.

XXVI.

But the Consul's brow was sad,
　　And the Consul's speech was low,
And darkly looked he at the wall,
　　And darkly at the foe.
' Their van will be upon us
　　Before the bridge goes down ;
And if they once may win the bridge,
　　What hope to save the town ? '

XXVII.

Then out spake brave Horatius,
　　The Captain of the Gate :
' To every man upon this earth
　　Death cometh soon or late.
And how can man die better
　　Than facing fearful odds,
For the ashes of his fathers,
　　And the temples of his Gods,

XXVIII.

' And for the tender mother
　　Who dandled him to rest,
And for the wife who nurses
　　His baby at her breast,
And for the holy maidens
　　Who feed the eternal flame,
To save them from false Sextus
　　That wrought the deed of shame ?

XXIX.

'Hew down the bridge, Sir Consul,
　With all the speed ye may;
I, with two more to help me,
　Will hold the foe in play.
In yon strait path a thousand
　May well be stopped by three.
Now who will stand on either hand,
　And keep the bridge with me?'

XXX.

Then out spake Spurius Lartius;
　A Ramnian proud was he:
'Lo, I will stand at thy right hand,
　And keep the bridge with thee.'
And out spake strong Herminius;
　Of Titian blood was he:
'I will abide on thy left side,
　And keep the bridge with thee.'

XXXI.

'Horatius,' quoth the Consul,
　'As thou sayest, so let it be.'
And straight against that great array
　Forth went the dauntless Three.
For Romans in Rome's quarrel
　Spared neither land nor gold,
Nor son nor wife, nor limb nor life,
　In the brave days of old.

D

XXXII.

Then none was for a party;
  Then all were for the state;
Then the great man helped the poor,
  And the poor man loved the great:
Then lands were fairly portioned;
  Then spoils were fairly sold:
The Romans were like brothers
  In the brave days of old.

XXXIII.

Now Roman is to Roman
  More hateful than a foe,
And the Tribunes beard the high,
  And the Fathers grind the low.
As we wax hot in faction,
  In battle we wax cold:
Wherefore men fight not as they fought
  In the brave days of old.

XXXIV.

Now while the Three were tightening
  Their harness on their backs,
The Consul was the foremost man
  To take in hand an axe:
And Fathers mixed with Commons
  Seized hatchet, bar, and crow,
And smote upon the planks above,
  And loosed the props below.

XXXV.

Meanwhile the Tuscan army,
  Right glorious to behold,
Came flashing back the noonday light,
Rank behind rank, like surges bright
  Of a broad sea of gold.
Four hundred trumpets sounded
  A peal of warlike glee,
As that great host, with measured tread,
And spears advanced, and ensigns spread,
Rolled slowly towards the bridge's head,
  Where stood the dauntless Three.

XXXVI.

The Three stood calm and silent,
  And looked upon the foes,
And a great shout of laughter
  From all the vanguard rose:
And forth three chiefs came spurring
  Before that deep array;
To earth they sprang, their swords they drew,
And lifted high their shields, and flew
  To win the narrow way;

XXXVII.

Aunus from green Tifernum,
  Lord of the Hill of Vines;
And Seius, whose eight hundred slaves
  Sicken in Ilva's mines;

And Picus, long to Clusium
　　Vassal in peace and war,
Who led to fight his Umbrian powers
From that grey crag where, girt with towers,
The fortress of Nequinum lowers
　　O'er the pale waves of Nar.

XXXVIII.

Stout Lartius hurled down Aunus
　　Into the stream beneath :
Herminius struck at Seius,
　　And clove him to the teeth :
At Picus brave Horatius
　　Darted one fiery thrust ;
And the proud Umbrian's gilded arms
　　Clashed in the bloody dust.

XXXIX.

Then Ocnus of Falerii
　　Rushed on the Roman Three ;
And Lausulus of Urgo,
　　The rover of the sea :
And Aruns of Volsinium,
　　Who slew the great wild boar,
The great wild boar that had his den
Amidst the reeds of Cosa's fen,
And wasted fields, and slaughtered men,
　　Along Albinia's shore.

XL.

Herminius smote down Aruns :
    Lartius laid Ocnus low :
Right to the heart of Lausulus
    Horatius sent a blow.
' Lie there,' he cried, ' fell pirate !
    No more, aghast and pale,
From Ostia's walls the crowd shall mark
The track of thy destroying bark.
No more Campania's hinds shall fly
To woods and caverns when they spy
    Thy thrice accursed sail.'

XLI.

But now no sound of laughter
    Was heard among the foes.
A wild and wrathful clamour
    From all the vanguard rose.
Six spears' lengths from the entrance
    Halted that deep array,
And for a space no man came forth
    To win the narrow way.

XLII.

But hark ! the cry is Astur.
    And lo ! the ranks divide;

And the great Lord of Luna
  Comes with his stately stride.
Upon his ample shoulders
  Clangs loud the fourfold shield,
And in his hand he shakes the brand
  Which none but he can wield.

XLIII.

He smiled on those bold Romans
  A smile serene and high ;
He eyed the flinching Tuscans,
  And scorn was in his eye.
Quoth he, 'The she-wolf's litter
  Stand savagely at bay :
But will ye dare to follow,
  If Astur clears the way ? '

XLIV.

Then, whirling up his broadsword
  With both hands to the height,
He rushed against Horatius,
  And smote with all his might.
With shield and blade Horatius
  Right deftly turned the blow.
The blow, though turned, came yet too nigh ;
It missed his helm, but gashed his thigh :
The Tuscans raised a joyful cry
  To see the red blood flow.

XLV.

He reeled, and on Herminius
    He leaned one breathing-space;
Then, like a wild cat mad with wounds,
    Sprang right at Astur's face.
Through teeth, and skull, and helmet
    So fierce a thrust he sped,
The good sword stood a hand-breadth out
    Behind the Tuscan's head.

XLVI.

And the great Lord of Luna
    Fell at that deadly stroke,
As falls on Mount Alvernus
    A thunder-smitten oak.
Far o'er the crashing forest
    The giant arms lie spread;
And the pale augurs, muttering low,
    Gaze on the blasted head.

XLVII.

On Astur's throat Horatius
    Right firmly pressed his heel,
And thrice and four times tugged amain,
    Ere he wrenched out the steel.
'And see,' he cried, 'the welcome,
    Fair guests, that waits you here!
What noble Lucumo comes next
    To taste our Roman cheer?'

XLVIII.

But at his haughty challenge
   A sullen murmur ran,
Mingled of wrath, and shame, and dread,
   Along that glittering van.
There lacked not men of prowess,
   Nor men of lordly race;
For all Etruria's noblest
   Were round the fatal place.

XLIX.

But all Etruria's noblest
   Felt their hearts sink to see
On the earth the bloody corpses,
   In the path the dauntless Three:
And, from the ghastly entrance
   Where those bold Romans stood,
All shrank, like boys who unaware,
Ranging the woods to start a hare,
Come to the mouth of the dark lair
Where, growling low, a fierce old bear
   Lies amidst bones and blood.

L.

Was none who would be foremost
   To lead such dire attack:
But those behind cried 'Forward!'
   And those before cried 'Back!'
And backward now and forward
   Wavers the deep array;

And on the tossing sea of steel,
To and fro the standards reel ;
And the victorious trumpet-peal
   Dies fitfully away.

LI.

Yet one man for one moment
   Stood out before the crowd ;
Well known was he to all the Three,
   And they gave him greeting loud,
' Now welcome, welcome, Sextus !
   Now welcome to thy home !
Why dost thou stay, and turn away ?
   Here lies the road to Rome.'

LII.

Thrice looked he at the city ;
   Thrice looked he at the dead ;
And thrice came on in fury,
   And thrice turned back in dread :
And, white with fear and hatred,
   Scowled at the narrow way
Where, wallowing in a pool of blood,
   The bravest Tuscans lay.

LIII.

But meanwhile axe and lever
   Have manfully been plied ;
And now the bridge hangs tottering
   Above the boiling tide.

'Come back, come back, Horatius!'
  Loud cried the Fathers all.
'Back, Lartius! back, Herminius!
  Back, ere the ruin fall!'

LIV.

Back darted Spurius Lartius;
  Herminius darted back:
And, as they passed, beneath their feet
  They felt the timbers crack.
But when they turned their faces,
  And on the farther shore
Saw brave Horatius stand alone,
  They would have crossed once more.

LV.

But with a crash like thunder
  Fell every loosened beam,
And, like a dam, the mighty wreck
  Lay right athwart the stream:
And a long shout of triumph
  Rose from the walls of Rome,
As to the highest turret-tops
  Was splashed the yellow foam.

LVI.

And, like a horse unbroken
  When first he feels the rein,
The furious river struggled hard,
  And tossed his tawny mane,

And burst the curb, and bounded,
   Rejoicing to be free,
And whirling down, in fierce career,
Battlement, and plank, and pier,
   Rushed headlong to the sea.

LVII.

Alone stood brave Horatius,
   But constant still in mind;
Thrice thirty thousand foes before,
   And the broad flood behind.
'Down with him!' cried false Sextus,
   With a smile on his pale face.
'Now yield thee,' cried Lars Porsena,
   'Now yield thee to our grace.'

LVIII.

Round turned he, as not deigning
   Those craven ranks to see;
Nought spake he to Lars Porsena,
   To Sextus nought spake he;
But he saw on Palatinus
   The white porch of his home;
And he spake to the noble river
   That rolls by the towers of Rome.

LIX.

'Oh, Tiber! father Tiber!
   To whom the Romans pray,

A Roman's life, a Roman's arms,
　　Take thou in charge this day!'
So he spake, and speaking sheathed
　　The good sword by his side,
And with his harness on his back,
　　Plunged headlong in the tide.

LX.

No sound of joy or sorrow
　　Was heard from either bank;
But friends and foes in dumb surprise,
With parted lips and straining eyes,
　　Stood gazing where he sank;
And when above the surges
　　They saw his crest appear,
All Rome sent forth a rapturous cry,
And even the ranks of Tuscany
　　Could scarce forbear to cheer.

LXI.

But fiercely ran the current,
　　Swollen high by months of rain:
And fast his blood was flowing;
　　And he was sore in pain,
And heavy with his armour,
　　And spent with changing blows:
And oft they thought him sinking,
　　But still again he rose.

LXII.

Never, I ween, did swimmer,
  In such an evil case,
Struggle through such a raging flood
  Safe to the landing place:
But his limbs were borne up bravely
  By the brave heart within,
And our good father Tiber
  Bore bravely up his chin.*

LXIII.

'Curse on him!' quoth false Sextus;
  'Will not the villain drown?
But for this stay, ere close of day
  We should have sacked the town!'
'Heaven help him!' quoth Lars Porsena,
  'And bring him safe to shore;
For such a gallant feat of arms
  Was never seen before.'

* 'Our ladye bare upp her chinne.'
              Ballad of Childe Waters.

'Never heavier man and horse
Stemmed a midnight torrent's force;
*   *   *   *   *   *
Yet, through good heart and our Lady's grace,
At length he gained the landing place.'
              Lay of the Last Minstrel, I.

LXIV.

And now he feels the bottom;
  Now on dry earth he stands;
Now round him throng the Fathers
  To press his gory hands;
And now, with shouts and clapping,
  And noise of weeping loud,
He enters through the River-Gate,
  Borne by the joyous crowd.

LXV.

They gave him of the corn-land,
  That was of public right,
As much as two strong oxen
  Could plough from morn till night;
And they made a molten image,
  And set it up on high,
And there it stands unto this day
  To witness if I lie.

LXVI.

It stands in the Comitium,
  Plain for all folk to see;
Horatius in his harness,
  Halting upon one knee:
And underneath is written,
  In letters all of gold,
How valiantly he kept the bridge
  In the brave days of old.

LXVII.

And still his name sounds stirring
  Unto the men of Rome,
As the trumpet-blast that cries to them
  To charge the Volscian home;
And wives still pray to Juno
  For boys with hearts as bold
As his who kept the bridge so well
  In the brave days of old.

LXVIII.

And in the nights of winter,
  When the cold north winds blow,
And the long howling of the wolves
  Is heard amidst the snow;
When round the lonely cottage
  Roars loud the tempest's din,
And the good logs of Algidus
  Roar louder yet within;

LXIX.

When the oldest cask is opened,
  And the largest lamp is lit;
When the chestnuts glow in the embers,
  And the kid turns on the spit;
When young and old in circle
  Around the firebrands close;
When the girls are weaving baskets,
  And the lads are shaping bows;

LXX.

When the goodman mends his armour,
And trims his helmet's plume;
When the goodwife's shuttle merrily
Goes flashing through the loom;
With weeping and with laughter
Still is the story told,
How well Horatius kept the bridge
In the brave days of old.

THE

BATTLE OF THE LAKE REGILLUS.

BATTLE OF THE LAKE REGILLUS.

THE following poem is supposed to have been produced about ninety years after the lay of Horatius.
Some persons mentioned in the lay of Horatius make
their appearance again, and some appellations and
epithets used in the lay of Horatius have been
purposely repeated : for, in an age of ballad-poetry,
it scarcely ever fails to happen, that certain phrases
come to be appropriated to certain men and things,
and are regularly applied to those men and things
by every minstrel.   Thus we find, both in the Homeric poems and in Hesiod, βίη Ἡρακληείη, περι-
κλύτος Ἀμφιγυήεις, διάκτορος Ἀργειφόντης, ἐπτάπυλος
Θήβη, Ἑλένης ἕνεκ᾽ ἠϋκόμοιο.   Thus, too, in our own
national songs, Douglas is almost always the
doughty Douglas : England is merry England : all
the gold is red ; and all the ladies are gay.

The principal distinction between the lay of
Horatius and the lay of the Lake Regillus is that
the former is meant to be purely Roman, while the
latter, though national in its general spirit, has a

slight tincture of Greek learning and of Greek
superstition.   The story of the Tarquins, as it has
come down to us, appears to have been compiled from
the works of several popular poets; and one, at
least, of those poets appears to have visited the
Greek colonies in Italy, if not Greece itself, and to
have had some acquaintance with the works of
Homer and Herodotus.   Many of the most striking
adventures of the house of Tarquin, before Lucretia
makes her appearance, have a Greek character.   The
Tarquins themselves are represented as Corinthian
nobles of the great house of the Bacchiadæ, driven
from their country by the tyranny of that Cypselus,
the tale of whose strange escape Herodotus has
related with incomparable simplicity and liveliness.*
Livy and Dionysius tell us that, when Tarquin the
Proud was asked what was the best mode of go-
verning a conquered city, he replied only by beating
down with his staff all the tallest poppies in his
garden.†   This is exactly what Herodotus, in the
passage to which reference has already been made,
relates of the counsel given to Periander, the son of
Cypselus.   The stratagem by which the town of
Gabii is brought under the power of the Tarquins
is, again, obviously copied from Herodotus.‡   The
embassy of the young Tarquins to the oracle at

* Herodotus, v. 92.   Livy, i. 34.   Dionysius, iii. 46.
† Livy, i. 54.   Dionysius, iv. 56.
‡ Herodotus, iii. 154.   Livy, i. 53.

Delphi is just such a story as would be told by a poet whose head was full of the Greek mythology; and the ambiguous answer returned by Apollo is in the exact style of the prophecies which, according to Herodotus, lured Crœsus to destruction. Then the character of the narrative changes. From the first mention of Lucretia to the retreat of Porsena nothing seems to be borrowed from foreign sources. The villany of Sextus, the suicide of his victim, the revolution, the death of the sons of Brutus, the defence of the bridge, Mucius burning his hand,* Clœlia swimming through Tiber, seem to be all strictly Roman. But when we have done with the Tuscan war, and enter upon the war with the Latines, we are again struck by the Greek air of the story. The Battle of the Lake Regillus is in all respects a Homeric battle, except that the combatants ride astride on their horses, instead of driving chariots. The mass of fighting men is hardly mentioned. The leaders single each other out, and engage hand to hand. The great object of the warriors on both sides is, as in the Iliad, to obtain possession of the spoils and bodies of the slain; and several circumstances are related which forcibly remind us of the great slaughter round the corpses of Sarpedon and Patroclus.

* M. de Pouilly attempted, a hundred and twenty years ago, to prove that the story of Mucius was of Greek origin: but he was signally confuted by the Abbé Sallier. See the *Mémoires de l'Académie des Inscriptions*, vi. 27. 66.

But there is one circumstance which deserves especial notice. Both the war of Troy and the war of Regillus were caused by the licentious passions of young princes, who were therefore peculiarly bound not to be sparing of their own persons in the day of battle. Now the conduct of Sextus at Regillus, as described by Livy, so exactly resembles that of Paris, as described at the beginning of the third book of the Iliad, that it is difficult to believe the resemblance accidental. Paris appears before the Trojan ranks, defying the bravest Greek to encounter him:

Τρωσὶν μὲν προμάχιζεν Ἀλέξανδρος θεοειδὴς,
. . . . Ἀργείων προκαλίζετο πάντας ἀρίστους,
ἀντίβιον μαχέσασθαι ἐν αἰνῇ δηϊοτῆτι.

Livy introduces Sextus in a similar manner: 'Ferocem juvenem Tarquinium, ostentantem se in prima exsulum acie.' Menelaus rushes to meet Paris. A Roman noble, eager for vengeance, spurs his horse towards Sextus. Both the guilty princes are instantly terror-stricken:

Τὸν δ' ὡς οὖν ἐνόησεν Ἀλέξανδρος θεοειδὴς
ἐν προμάχοισι φανέντα, κατεπλήγη φίλον ἦτορ·
ἂψ δ' ἑτάρων εἰς ἔθνος ἐχάζετο κῆρ' ἀλεείνων.

'Tarquinius,' says Livy, 'retro in agmen suorum infenso cessit hosti.' If this be a fortuitous coincidence, it is one of the most extraordinary in literature.

In the following poem, therefore, images and incidents have been borrowed, not merely without scruple, but on principle, from the incomparable battle-pieces of Homer.

The popular belief at Rome, from an early period, seems to have been that the event of the great day of Regillus was decided by supernatural agency. Castor and Pollux, it was said, had fought, armed and mounted, at the head of the legions of the commonwealth, and had afterwards carried the news of the victory with incredible speed to the city. The well in the Forum at which they had alighted was pointed out. Near the well rose their ancient temple. A great festival was kept to their honour on the Ides of Quintilis, supposed to be the anniversary of the battle; and on that day sumptuous sacrifices were offered to them at the public charge. One spot on the margin of Lake Regillus was regarded during many ages with superstitious awe. A mark, resembling in shape a horse's hoof, was discernible in the volcanic rock; and this mark was believed to have been made by one of the celestial chargers.

How the legend originated cannot now be ascertained: but we may easily imagine several ways in which it might have originated; nor is it at all necessary to suppose, with Julius Frontinus, that two young men were dressed up by the Dictator to personate the sons of Leda. It is probable that

Livy is correct when he says that the Roman general, in the hour of peril, vowed a temple to Castor.
If so, nothing could be more natural than that the
multitude should ascribe the victory to the favour
of the Twin Gods. When such was the prevailing
sentiment, any man who chose to declare that, in
the midst of the confusion and slaughter, he had
seen two godlike forms on white horses scattering
the Latines, would find ready credence. We know,
indeed, that, in modern times, a very similar story
actually found credence among a people much more
civilised than the Romans of the fifth century before
Christ. A chaplain of Cortes, writing about thirty
years after the conquest of Mexico, in an age of
printing presses, libraries, universities, scholars,
logicians, jurists, and statesmen, had the face to
assert that, in one engagement against the Indians,
Saint James had appeared on a grey horse at the
head of the Castilian adventurers. Many of those
adventurers were living when this lie was printed.
One of them, honest Bernal Diaz, wrote an account
of the expedition. He had the evidence of his own
senses against the legend; but he seems to have
distrusted even the evidence of his own senses. He
says that he was in the battle, and that he saw a
grey horse with a man on his back, but that the
man was, to his thinking, Francesco de Morla, and
not the ever-blessed apostle Saint James. 'Nevertheless,' Bernal adds, 'it may be that the person

on the grey horse was the glorious apostle Saint
James, and that I, sinner that I am, was unworthy
to see him.' The Romans of the age of Cincinnatus
were probably quite as credulous as the Spanish
subjects of Charles the Fifth. It is therefore con-
ceivable that the appearance of Castor and Pollux
may have become an article of faith before the
generation which had fought at Regillus had passed
away. Nor could anything be more natural than
that the poets of the next age should embellish this
story, and make the celestial horsemen bear the
tidings of victory to Rome.

Many years after the temple of the Twin Gods
had been built in the Forum, an important addition
was made to the ceremonial by which the state annually testified its gratitude for their protection.
Quintus Fabius and Publius Decius were elected
Censors at a momentous crisis. It had become ab-
solutely necessary that the classification of the
citizens should be revised. On that classification
depended the distribution of political power.
Party-spirit ran high; and the republic seemed
to be in danger of falling under the dominion
either of a narrow oligarchy or of an ignorant
and headstrong rabble. Under such circumstances, the most illustrious patrician and the
most illustrious plebeian of the age were intrusted
with the office of arbitrating between the angry
factions; and they performed their arduous task

to the satisfaction of all honest and reasonable men.

One of their reforms was a remodelling of the equestrian order ; and, having effected this reform, they determined to give to their work a sanction derived from religion. In the chivalrous societies of modern times, societies which have much more than may at first sight appear in common with the equestrian order of Rome, it has been usual to invoke the special protection of some Saint, and to observe his day with peculiar solemnity. Thus the Companions of the Garter wear the image of Saint George depending from their collars, and meet, on great occasions, in Saint George's Chapel. Thus, when Lewis the Fourteenth instituted a new order of chivalry for the rewarding of military merit, he commended it to the favour of his own glorified ancestor and patron, and decreed that all the members of the fraternity should meet at the royal palace on the feast of Saint Lewis, should attend the king to chapel, should hear mass, and should subsequently hold their great annual assembly. There is a considerable resemblance between this rule of the order of Saint Lewis and the rule which Fabius and Decius made respecting the Roman knights. It was ordained that a grand muster and inspection of the equestrian body should be part of the ceremonial performed, on the anniversary of the battle of Regillus, in honour of Castor and

Pollux, the two equestrian Gods. All the knights, clad in purple and crowned with olive, were to meet at a temple of Mars in the suburbs. Thence they were to ride in state to the Forum, where the temple of the Twins stood. This pageant was, during several centuries, considered as one of the most splendid sights of Rome. In the time of Dionysius the cavalcade sometimes consisted of five thousand horsemen, all persons of fair repute and easy fortune.*

There can be no doubt that the Censors who instituted this august ceremony acted in concert with the Pontiffs to whom, by the constitution of Rome, the superintendence of the public worship belonged; and it is probable that those high religious functionaries were, as usual, fortunate enough to find in their books or traditions some warrant for the innovation.

The following poem is supposed to have been made for this great occasion. Songs, we know, were chanted at the religious festivals of Rome from an early period; indeed from so early a period, that some of the sacred verses were popularly ascribed to Numa, and were utterly unintelligible in the age of Augustus. In the Second Punic War

* See Livy, ix. 46. Val. Max. ii. 2. Aurel. Vict. De Viris Illustribus, 32. Dionysius, vi. 13. Plin. Hist. Nat. xv. 5. See also the singularly ingenious chapter in Niebuhr's posthumous volume, *Die Censur des Q. Fabius und P. Decius.*

a great feast was held in honour of Juno, and a song was sung in her praise. This song was extant when Livy wrote; and, though exceedingly rugged and uncouth, seemed to him not wholly destitute of merit.* A song, as we learn from Horace,† was part of the established ritual at the great Secular Jubilee. It is therefore likely that the Censors and Pontiffs, when they had resolved to add a grand procession of knights to the other solemnities annually performed on the Ides of Quintilis, would call in the aid of a poet. Such a poet would naturally take for his subject the battle of Regillus, the appearance of the Twin Gods, and the institution of their festival. He would find abundant materials in the ballads of his predecessors; and he would make free use of the scanty stock of Greek learning which he had himself acquired. He would probably introduce some wise and holy Pontiff enjoining the magnificent ceremonial which, after a long interval, had at length been adopted. If the poem succeeded, many persons would commit it to memory. Parts of it would be sung to the pipe at banquets. It would be peculiarly interesting to the great Posthumian House, which numbered among its many images that of the Dictator Aulus, the hero of Regillus. The orator who, in the following generation, pronounced the funeral panegyric over the remains of

* Livy, xxvii. 37. † Hor. Carmen Seculare.

Lucius Posthumius Megellus, thrice Consul, would borrow largely from the lay; and thus some passages, much disfigured, would probably find their way into the chronicles which were afterwards in the hands of Dionysius and Livy.

Antiquaries differ widely as to the situation of the field of battle. The opinion of those who suppose that the armies met near Cornufelle, between Frascati and the Monte Porzio, is at least plausible, and has been followed in the poem.

As to the details of the battle, it has not been thought desirable to adhere minutely to the accounts which have come down to us. Those accounts, indeed, differ widely from each other, and, in all probability, differ as widely from the ancient poem from which they were originally derived.

It is unnecessary to point out the obvious imitations of the Iliad, which have been purposely introduced.

THE

BATTLE OF THE LAKE REGILLUS.

A LAY SUNG AT THE FEAST OF CASTOR AND POLLUX
ON THE IDES OF QUINTILIS,
IN THE YEAR OF THE CITY CCCCLI.

I.

Ho, trumpets, sound a war-note!
 Ho, lictors, clear the way!
The Knights will ride, in all their pride,
 Along the streets to-day.
To-day the doors and windows
 Are hung with garlands all,
From Castor in the Forum,
 To Mars without the wall.
Each Knight is robed in purple,
 With olive each is crowned;
A gallant war-horse under each
 Paws haughtily the ground.
While flows the Yellow River,
 While stands the Sacred Hill,
The proud Ides of Quintilis
 Shall have such honour still.

Gay are the Martian Kalends:
  December's Nones are gay:
But the proud Ides, when the squadron rides,
  Shall be Rome's whitest day.

II.

Unto the Great Twin Brethren
  We keep this solemn feast.
Swift, swift, the Great Twin Brethren
  Came spurring from the east.
They came o'er wild Parthenius
  Tossing in waves of pine,
O'er Cirrha's dome, o'er Adria's foam,
  O'er purple Apennine,
From where with flutes and dances
  Their ancient mansion rings,
In lordly Lacedæmon,
  The City of two kings,
To where, by Lake Regillus,
  Under the Porcian height,
All in the lands of Tusculum,
  Was fought the glorious fight.

III.

Now on the place of slaughter
  Are cots and sheepfolds seen,
And rows of vines, and fields of wheat,
  And apple-orchards green;

The swine crush the big acorns
 That fall from Corne's oaks.
Upon the turf by the Fair Fount
 The reaper's pottage smokes.
The fisher baits his angle ;
 The hunter twangs his bow ;
Little they think on those strong limbs
 That moulder deep below.
Little they think how sternly
 That day the trumpets pealed ;
How in the slippery swamp of blood
 Warrior and war-horse reeled ;
How wolves came with fierce gallop,
 And crows on eager wings,
To tear the flesh of captains,
 And peck the eyes of kings ;
How thick the dead lay scattered
 Under the Porcian height ;
How through the gates of Tusculum
 Raved the wild stream of flight ;
And how the Lake Regillus
 Bubbled with crimson foam,
What time the Thirty Cities
 Came forth to war with Rome.

IV.

But, Roman, when thou standest
 Upon that holy ground,
Look thou with heed on the dark rock
 That girds the dark lake round.

F

So shalt thou see a hoof-mark
 Stamped deep into the flint:
It was no hoof of mortal steed
 That made so strange a dint:
There to the Great Twin Brethren
 Vow thou thy vows, and pray
That they, in tempest and in fight,
 Will keep thy head alway.

V.

Since last the Great Twin Brethren
 Of mortal eyes were seen,
Have years gone by an hundred
 And fourscore and thirteen.
That summer a Virginius
 Was Consul first in place;
The second was stout Aulus,
 Of the Posthumian race.
The Herald of the Latines
 From Gabii came in state:
The Herald of the Latines
 Passed through Rome's Eastern Gate:
The Herald of the Latines
 Did in our Forum stand;
And there he did his office,
 A sceptre in his hand.

VI.

' Hear, Senators and people
 Of the good town of Rome,

The Thirty Cities charge you
　　To bring the Tarquins home :
And if ye still be stubborn,
　　To work the Tarquins wrong,
The Thirty Cities warn you,
　　Look that your walls be strong.'

VII.

Then spake the Consul Aulus,
　　He spake a bitter jest :
' Once the jays sent a message
　　Unto the eagle's nest :—
Now yield thou up thine eyrie
　　Unto the carrion-kite,
Or come forth valiantly, and face
　　The jays in deadly fight.—
Forth looked in wrath the eagle ;
　　And carrion-kite and jay,
Soon as they saw his beak and claw,
　　Fled screaming far away.'

VIII.

The Herald of the Latines
　　Hath hied him back in state :
The Fathers of the City
　　Are met in high debate.
Then spake the elder Consul,
　　An ancient man and wise :
' Now hearken, Conscript Fathers,
　　To that which I advise.

In seasons of great peril
　'Tis good that one bear sway;
Then choose we a Dictator,
　Whom all men shall obey.
Camerium knows how deeply
　The sword of Aulus bites,
And all our city calls him
　The man of seventy fights.
Then let him be Dictator
　For six months and no more,
And have a Master of the Knights,
　And axes twenty-four.'

IX.

So Aulus was Dictator,
　The man of seventy fights;
He made Æbutius Elva
　His Master of the Knights.
On the third morn thereafter,
　At dawning of the day,
Did Aulus and Æbutius
　Set forth with their array.
Sempronius Atratinus
　Was left in charge at home
With boys, and with grey-headed men,
　To keep the walls of Rome.
Hard by the Lake Regillus
　Our camp was pitched at night:
Eastward a mile the Latines lay,
　Under the Porcian height.

Far over hill and valley
  Their mighty host was spread;
And with their thousand watch-fires
  The midnight sky was red.

X.

Up rose the golden morning
  Over the Porcian height,
The proud Ides of Quintilis
  Marked evermore with white.
Not without secret trouble
  Our bravest saw the foes;
For girt by threescore thousand spears,
  The thirty standards rose.
From every warlike city
  That boasts the Latian name,
Foredoomed to dogs and vultures,
  That gallant army came;
From Setia's purple vineyards,
  From Norba's ancient wall,
From the white streets of Tusculum,
  The proudest town of all;
From where the Witch's Fortress
  O'erhangs the dark-blue seas;
From the still glassy lake that sleeps
  Beneath Aricia's trees —
Those trees in whose dim shadow
  The ghastly priest doth reign,
The priest who slew the slayer,
  And shall himself be slain;

From the drear banks of Ufens,
   Where flights of marsh-fowl play,
And buffaloes lie wallowing
   Through the hot summer's day ;
From the gigantic watch-towers,
   No work of earthly men,
Whence Cora's sentinels o'erlook
   The never-ending fen ;
From the Laurentian jungle,
   The wild hog's reedy home ;
From the green steeps whence Anio leaps
   In floods of snow-white foam.

XI.

Aricia, Cora, Norba,
   Velitræ, with the might
Of Setia and of Tusculum,
   Were marshalled on the right :
The leader was Mamilius,
   Prince of the Latian name ;
Upon his head a helmet
   Of red gold shone like flame :
High on a gallant charger
   Of dark-grey hue he rode ;
Over his gilded armour
   A vest of purple flowed,
Woven in the land of sunrise
   By Syria's dark-browed daughters,
And by the sails of Carthage brought
   Far o'er the southern waters.

XII.

Lavinium and Laurentum
  Had on the left their post,
With all the banners of the marsh,
  And banners of the coast.
Their leader was false Sextus,
  That wrought the deed of shame :
With restless pace and haggard face
  To his last field he came.
Men said he saw strange visions
  Which none beside might see,
And that strange sounds were in his ears
  Which none might hear but he.
A woman fair and stately,
  But pale as are the dead,
Oft through the watches of the night
  Sat spinning by his bed.
And as she plied the distaff,
  In a sweet voice and low,
She sang of great old houses,
  And fights fought long ago.
So spun she, and so sang she,
  Until the east was grey,
Then pointed to her bleeding breast,
  And shrieked, and fled away.

XIII.

But in the centre thickest
  Were ranged the shields of foes,
And from the centre loudest
  The cry of battle rose.

There Tibur marched and Pedum
　　Beneath proud Tarquin's rule,
And Ferentinum of the rock,
　　And Gabii of the pool.
There rode the Volscian succours:
　　There, in a dark stern ring,
The Roman exiles gathered close
　　Around the ancient king.
Though white as Mount Soracte,
　　When winter nights are long,
His beard flowed down o'er mail and belt,
　　His heart and hand were strong:
Under his hoary eyebrows
　　Still flashed forth quenchless rage,
And, if the lance shook in his gripe,
　　'Twas more with hate than age.
Close at his side was Titus
　　On an Apulian steed,
Titus, the youngest Tarquin,
　　Too good for such a breed.

XIV.

Now on each side the leaders
　　Give signal for the charge;
And on each side the footmen
　　Strode on with lance and targe;
And on each side the horsemen
　　Struck their spurs deep in gore;
And front to front the armies
　　Met with a mighty roar:

And under that great battle
  The earth with blood was red;
And, like the Pomptine fog at morn,
  The dust hung overhead;
And louder still and louder
  Rose from the darkened field
The braying of the war-horns,
  The clang of sword and shield,
The rush of squadrons sweeping
  Like whirlwinds o'er the plain,
The shouting of the slayers,
  And screeching of the slain.

XV.

False Sextus rode out foremost:
  His look was high and bold;
His corslet was of bison's hide,
  Plated with steel and gold.
As glares the famished eagle
  From the Digentian rock
On a choice lamb that bounds alone
  Before Bandusia's flock,
Herminius glared on Sextus,
  And came with eagle speed,
Herminius on black Auster,
  Brave champion on brave steed;
In his right hand the broadsword
  That kept the bridge so well,
And on his helm the crown he won
  When proud Fidenæ fell.

Woe to the maid whose lover
   Shall cross his path to-day!
False Sextus saw, and trembled,
   And turned, and fled away.
As turns, as flies, the woodman
   In the Calabrian brake,
When through the reeds gleams the round eye
   Of that fell speckled snake;
So turned, so fled, false Sextus,
   And hid him in the rear,
Behind the dark Lavinian ranks,
   Bristling with crest and spear.

XVI.

But far to north Æbutius,
   The Master of the Knights,
Gave Tubero of Norba
   To feed the Porcian kites.
Next under those red horse-hoofs
   Flaccus of Setia lay;
Better had he been pruning
   Among his elms that day.
Mamilius saw the slaughter,
   And tossed his golden crest,
And towards the Master of the Knights
   Through the thick battle pressed.
Æbutius smote Mamilius
   So fiercely on the shield
That the great lord of Tusculum
   Well nigh rolled on the field.

Mamilius smote Æbutius,
  With a good aim and true,
Just where the neck and shoulder join,
  And pierced him through and through ;
And brave Æbutius Elva
  Fell swooning to the ground :
But a thick wall of bucklers
  Encompassed him around.
His clients from the battle
  Bare him some little space,
And filled a helm from the dark lake,
  And bathed his brow and face ;
And when at last he opened
  His swimming eyes to light,
Men say, the earliest word he spake
  Was, ' Friends, how goes the fight ? '

XVII.

But meanwhile in the centre
  Great deeds of arms were wrought ;
There Aulus the Dictator
  And there Valerius fought.
Aulus with his good broadsword
  A bloody passage cleared
To where, amidst the thickest foes,
  He saw the long white beard.
Flat lighted that good broadsword
  Upon proud Tarquin's head.
He dropped the lance : he dropped the reins :
  He fell as fall the dead.

Down Aulus springs to slay him,
   With eyes like coals of fire ;
But faster Titus hath sprung down,
   And hath bestrode his sire.
Latian captains, Roman knights,
   Fast down to earth they spring,
And hand to hand they fight on foot
   Around the ancient king.
First Titus gave tall Cæso
   A death wound in the face ;
Tall Cæso was the bravest man
   Of the brave Fabian race :
Aulus slew Rex of Gabii,
   The priest of Juno's shrine :
Valerius smote down Julius,
   Of Rome's great Julian line ;
Julius, who left his mansion
   High on the Velian hill,
And through all turns of weal and woe
   Followed proud Tarquin still.
Now right across proud Tarquin
   A corpse was Julius laid ;
And Titus groaned with rage and grief,
   And at Valerius made.
Valerius struck at Titus,
   And lopped off half his crest ;
But Titus stabbed Valerius
   A span deep in the breast.
Like a mast snapped by the tempest,
   Valerius reeled and fell.
Ah ! woe is me for the good house
   That loves the people well !

Then shouted loud the Latines;
  And with one rush they bore
The struggling Romans backward
  Three lances' length and more:
And up they took proud Tarquin,
  And laid him on a shield,
And four strong yeomen bare him,
  Still senseless, from the field.

XVIII.

But fiercer grew the fighting
  Around Valerius dead;
For Titus dragged him by the foot,
  And Aulus by the head.
'On, Latines, on!' quoth Titus,
  'See how the rebels fly!'
'Romans, stand firm!' quoth Aulus,
  'And win this fight or die!
They must not give Valerius
  To raven and to kite;
For aye Valerius loathed the wrong,
  And aye upheld the right:
And for your wives and babies
  In the front rank he fell.
Now play the men for the good house
  That loves the people well!'

XIX.

Then tenfold round the body
  The roar of battle rose,

Like the roar of a burning forest,
　　When a strong north wind blows.
Now backward, and now forward,
　　Rocked furiously the fray,
Till none could see Valerius,
　　And none wist where he lay.
For shivered arms and ensigns
　　Were heaped there in a mound,
And corpses stiff, and dying men
　　That writhed and gnawed the ground ;
And wounded horses kicking,
　　And snorting purple foam :
Right well did such a couch befit
　　A Consular of Rome.

XX.

But north looked the Dictator ;
　　North looked he long and hard ;
And spake to Caius Cossus,
　　The Captain of his Guard ;
‘ Caius, of all the Romans
　　Thou hast the keenest sight ;
Say, what through yonder storm of dust
　　Comes from the Latian right ? ’

XXI.

Then answered Caius Cossus :
　　‘ I see an evil sight ;
The banner of proud Tusculum
　　Comes from the Latian right ;

I see the plumed horsemen;
  And far before the rest
I see the dark-grey charger,
  I see the purple vest ;
I see the golden helmet
  That shines far off like flame ;
So ever rides Mamilius,
  Prince of the Latian name.'

XXII.

' Now hearken, Caius Cossus :
  Spring on thy horse's back ;
Ride as the wolves of Apennine
  Were all upon thy track ;
Haste to our southward battle :
  And never draw thy rein
Until thou find Herminius,
  And bid him come amain.'

XXIII.

So Aulus spake, and turned him
  Again to that fierce strife ;
And Caius Cossus mounted,
  And rode for death and life.
Loud clanged beneath his horse-hoofs
  The helmets of the dead,
And many a curdling pool of blood
  Splashed him from heel to head.
So came he far to southward,
  Where fought the Roman host,

Against the banners of the marsh
  And banners of the coast.
Like corn before the sickle
  The stout Lavinians fell,
Beneath the edge of the true sword
  That kept the bridge so well.

XXIV.

'Herminius! Aulus greets thee;
  He bids thee come with speed,
To help our central battle;
  For sore is there our need.
There wars the youngest Tarquin,
  And there the Crest of Flame,
The Tusculan Mamilius,
  Prince of the Latian name.
Valerius hath fallen fighting
  In front of our array:
And Aulus of the seventy fields
  Alone upholds the day.'

XXV.

Herminius beat his bosom:
  But never a word he spake.
He clapped his hand on Auster's mane:
  He gave the reins a shake,
Away, away went Auster,
  Like an arrow from the bow:
Black Auster was the fleetest steed
  From Aufidus to Po.

XXVI.

Right glad were all the Romans
   Who, in that hour of dread,
Against great odds bare up the war
   Around Valerius dead,
When from the south the cheering
   Rose with a mighty swell ;
' Herminius comes, Herminius,
   Who kept the bridge so well ! '

XXVII.

Mamilius spied Herminius,
   And dashed across the way.
' Herminius ! I have sought thee
   Through many a bloody day.
One of us two, Herminius,
   Shall never more go home.
I will lay on for Tusculum,
   And lay thou on for Rome ! '

XXVIII.

All round them paused the battle,
   While met in mortal fray
The Roman and the Tusculan,
   The horses black and grey.
Herminius smote Mamilius
   Through breast-plate and through breast ;
And fast flowed out the purple blood
   Over the purple vest.
Mamilius smote Herminius
   Through head-piece and through head ;

G

And side by side those chiefs of pride
   Together fell down dead.
Down fell they dead together
   In a great lake of gore;
And still stood all who saw them fall
   While men might count a score.

XXIX.

Fast, fast, with heels wild spurning,
   The dark-grey charger fled:
He burst through ranks of fighting men;
   He sprang o'er heaps of dead.
His bridle far out-streaming,
   His flanks all blood and foam,
He sought the southern mountains,
   The mountains of his home.
The pass was steep and rugged,
   The wolves they howled and whined;
But he ran like a whirlwind up the pass,
   And he left the wolves behind.
Through many a startled hamlet
   Thundered his flying feet;
He rushed through the gate of Tusculum,
   He rushed up the long white street;
He rushed by tower and temple,
   And paused not from his race
Till he stood before his master's door
   In the stately market-place.
And straightway round him gathered
   A pale and trembling crowd,

And when they knew him, cries of rage
    Brake forth, and wailing loud :
And women rent their tresses
    For their great prince's fall;
And old men girt on their old swords,
    And went to man the wall.

XXX.

But, like a graven image,
    Black Auster kept his place,
And ever wistfully he looked
    Into his master's face.
The raven-mane that daily,
    With pats and fond caresses,
The young Herminia washed and combed,
    And twined in even tresses,
And decked with coloured ribands
    From her own gay attire,
Hung sadly o'er her father's corpse
    In carnage and in mire.
Forth with a shout sprang Titus,
    And seized black Auster's reign.
Then Aulus sware a fearful oath,
    And ran at him amain.
'The furies of thy brother
    With me and mine abide,
If one of your accursed house
    Upon black Auster ride!'
As on an Alpine watch-tower
    From heaven comes down the flame,

Full on the neck of Titus
   The blade of Aulus came:
And out the red blood spouted,
   In a wide arch and tall,
As spouts a fountain in the court
   Of some rich Capuan's hall.
The knees of all the Latines
   Were loosened with dismay
When dead, on dead Herminius,
   The bravest Tarquin lay.

XXXI.

And Aulus the Dictator
   Stroked Auster's raven mane,
With heed he looked unto the girths,
   With heed unto the rein.
'Now bear me well, black Auster,
   Into yon thick array;
And thou and I will have revenge
   For thy good lord this day.'

XXXII.

So spake he; and was buckling
   Tighter black Auster's band,
When he was aware of a princely pair
   That rode at his right hand.
So like they were, no mortal
   Might one from other know:
White as snow their armour was:
   Their steeds were white as snow.

Never on earthly anvil
  Did such rare armour gleam;
And never did such gallant steeds
  Drink of an earthly stream.

XXXIII.

And all who saw them trembled,
  And pale grew every cheek;
And Aulus the Dictator
  Scarce gathered voice to speak.
'Say by what name men call you?
  What city is your home?
And wherefore ride ye in such guise
  Before the ranks of Rome?'

XXXIV.

'By many names men call us;
  In many lands we dwell:
Well Samothracia knows us;
  Cyrene knows us well.
Our house in gay Tarentum
  Is hung each morn with flowers:
High o'er the masts of Syracuse
  Our marble portal towers;
But by the proud Eurotas
  Is our dear native home;
And for the right we come to fight
  Before the ranks of Rome.'

XXXV.

So answered those strange horsemen,
   And each couched low his spear;
And forthwith all the ranks of Rome
   Were bold, and of good cheer:
And on the thirty armies
   Came wonder and affright,
And Ardea wavered on the left,
   And Cora on the right.
' Rome to the charge!' cried Aulus;
   ' The foe begins to yield!
Charge for the hearth of Vesta!
   Charge for the Golden Shield!
Let no man stop to plunder,
   But slay, and slay, and slay;
The Gods who live for ever
   Are on our side to-day.'

XXXVI.

Then the fierce trumpet-flourish
   From earth to heaven arose,
The kites know well the long stern swell
   That bids the Romans close.
Then the good sword of Aulus
   Was lifted up to slay:
Then, like a crag down Apennine,
   Rushed Auster through the fray.
But under those strange horsemen
   Still thicker lay the slain;
And after those strange horses
   Black Auster toiled in vain.

Behind them Rome's long battle
  Came rolling on the foe,
Ensigns dancing wild above,
  Blades all in line below.
So comes the Po in flood-time
  Upon the Celtic plain :
So comes the squall, blacker than night,
  Upon the Adrian main.
Now, by our Sire Quirinus,
  It was a goodly sight
To see the thirty standards
  Swept down the tide of flight.
So flies the spray of Adria
  When the black squall doth blow,
So corn-sheaves in the flood-time
  Spin down the whirling Po.
False Sextus to the mountains
  Turned first his horse's head ;
And fast fled Ferentinum,
  And fast Lanuvium fled.
The horsemen of Nomentum
  Spurred hard out of the fray ;
The footmen of Velitræ
  Threw shield and spear away.
And underfoot was trampled,
  Amidst the mud and gore,
The banner of proud Tusculum,
  That never stooped before :
And down went Flavius Faustus,
  Who led his stately ranks
From where the apple blossoms wave
  On Anio's echoing banks,

And Tullus of Arpinum,
　Chief of the Volscian aids,
And Metius with the long fair curls,
　The love of Anxur's maids,
And the white head of Vulso,
　The great Arician seer,
And Nepos of Laurentum,
　The hunter of the deer;
And in the back false Sextus
　Felt the good Roman steel,
And wriggling in the dust he died,
　Like a worm beneath the wheel:
And fliers and pursuers
　Were mingled in a mass;
And far away the battle
　Went roaring through the pass.

XXXVII.

Sempronius Atratinus
　Sate in the Eastern Gate,
Beside him were three Fathers,
　Each in his chair of state;
Fabius, whose nine stout grandsons
　That day were in the field,
And Manlius, eldest of the Twelve
　Who kept the Golden Shield;
And Sergius, the High Pontiff,
　For wisdom far renowned;
In all Etruria's colleges
　Was no such Pontiff found.

And all around the portal,
    And high above the wall,
Stood a great throng of people,
    But sad and silent all ;
Young lads, and stooping elders
    That might not bear the mail,
Matrons with lips that quivered,
    And maids with faces pale.
Since the first gleam of daylight,
    Sempronius had not ceased
To listen for the rushing
    Of horse-hoofs from the east.
The mist of eve was rising,
    The sun was hastening down,
When he was aware of a princely pair
    Fast pricking towards the town.
So like they were, man never
    Saw twins so like before ;
Red with gore their armour was,
    Their steeds were red with gore.

XXXVIII.

' Hail to the great Asylum !
    Hail to the hill-tops seven !
Hail to the fire that burns for aye,
    And the shield that fell from heaven !
This day, by Lake Regillus,
    Under the Porcian height,
All in the lands of Tusculum
    Was fought a glorious fight,

To-morrow your Dictator
　　Shall bring in triumph home
The spoils of thirty cities
　　To deck the shrines of Rome!'

XXXIX.

Then burst from that great concourse
　　A shout that shook the towers,
And some ran north, and some ran south,
　　Crying, 'The day is ours!'
But on rode these strange horsemen,
　　With slow and lordly pace;
And none who saw their bearing
　　Durst ask their name or race.
On rode they to the Forum,
　　While laurel-boughs and flowers,
From house-tops and from windows,
　　Fell on their crests in showers.
When they drew nigh to Vesta,
　　They vaulted down amain,
And washed their horses in the well
　　That springs by Vesta's fane.
And straight again they mounted,
　　And rode to Vesta's door;
Then, like a blast, away they passed,
　　And no man saw them more.

XL.

And all the people trembled,
　　And pale grew every cheek;

And Sergius the High Pontiff
  Alone found voice to speak :
' The gods who live for ever
  Have fought for Rome to-day !
These be the Great Twin Brethren
  To whom the Dorians pray.
Back comes the Chief in triumph,
  Who, in the hour of fight,
Hath seen the Great Twin Brethren
  In harness on his right.
Safe comes the ship to haven,
  Through billows and through gales,
If once the Great Twin Brethren
  Sit shining on the sails.
Wherefore they washed their horses
  In Vesta's holy well,
Wherefore they rode to Vesta's door,
  I know, but may not tell.
Here, hard by Vesta's Temple,
  Build we a stately dome
Unto the Great Twin Brethren
  Who fought so well for Rome.
And when the months returning
  Bring back this day of fight,
The proud Ides of Quintilis,
  Marked evermore with white,
Unto the Great Twin Brethren
  Let all the people throng,
With chaplets and with offerings,
  With music and with song ;
And let the doors and windows
  Be hung with garlands all,

And let the Knights be summoned
  To Mars without the wall:
Thence let them ride in purple
  With joyous trumpet-sound,
Each mounted on his war-horse,
  And each with olive crowned;
And pass in solemn order
  Before the sacred dome,
Where dwell the Great Twin Brethren
  Who fought so well for Rome!'

VIRGINIA.

VIRGINIA.

A COLLECTION consisting exclusively of war-songs would give an imperfect, or rather an erroneous, notion of the spirit of the old Latin ballads. The Patricians, during more than a century after the expulsion of the Kings, held all the high military commands. A Plebeian, even though, like Lucius Siccius, he were distinguished by his valour and knowledge of war, could serve only in subordinate posts. A minstrel, therefore, who wished to celebrate the early triumphs of his country, could hardly take any but Patricians for his heroes. The warriors who are mentioned in the two preceding lays, Horatius, Lartius, Herminius, Aulus Posthumius, Æbutius Elva, Sempronius Atratinus, Valerius Poplicola, were all members of the dominant order; and a poet who was singing their praises, whatever his own political opinions might be, would naturally abstain from insulting the class to which they belonged, and from reflecting on the system which had placed such men at the head of the legions of the Commonwealth.

But there was a class of compositions in which

the great families were by no means so courteously treated. No parts of early Roman history are richer with poetical colouring than those which relate to the long contest between the privileged houses and the commonalty. The population of Rome was, from a very early period, divided into hereditary castes, which, indeed, readily united to repel foreign enemies, but which regarded each other, during many years, with bitter animosity. Between those castes there was a barrier hardly less strong than that which, at Venice, parted the members of the Great Council from their countrymen. In some respects, indeed, the line which separated an Icilius or a Duilius from a Posthumius or a Fabius was even more deeply marked than that which separated the rower of a gondola from a Contarini or a Morosini. At Venice the distinction was merely civil. At Rome it was both civil and religious. Among the grievances under which the Plebeians suffered, three were felt as peculiarly severe. They were excluded from the highest magistracies; they were excluded from all share in the public lands; and they were ground down to the dust by partial and barbarous legislation touching pecuniary contracts. The ruling class in Rome was a monied class; and it made and administered the laws with a view solely to its own interest. Thus the relation between lender and borrower was mixed up with the relation between sovereign and subject. The great men held a large portion of the community in dependence by means of advances at enormous usury. The law of debt, framed by creditors, and for the protection of creditors, was the most horrible that has ever been known among men. The liberty, and even the life, of the insolvent were at the mercy of the Patrician money-lenders. Children often became slaves in consequence of the misfortunes of their parents. The debtor was imprisoned, not in a public gaol under the care of impartial public functionaries, but in a private workhouse belonging to the creditor. Frightful stories were told respecting these dungeons. It was said that torture and brutal violation were common; that tight stocks, heavy chains, scanty measures of food, were used to punish wretches guilty of nothing but poverty; and that brave soldiers, whose breasts were covered with honourable scars, were often marked still more deeply on the back by the scourges of high-born usurers.

The Plebeians were, however, not wholly without constitutional rights. From an early period they had been admitted to some share of political power. They were enrolled each in his century, and were allowed a share, considerable though not proportioned to their numerical strength, in the disposal of those high dignities from which they were themselves excluded. Thus their position bore some

resemblance to that of the Irish Catholics during
the interval between the year 1792 and the year
1829.   The Plebeians had also the privilege of annually appointing officers, named Tribunes, who had
no active share in the government of the Commonwealth, but who, by degrees, acquired a power for-
midable even to the ablest and most resolute Consuls
and Dictators.   The person of the Tribune was in-
violable ; and, though he could directly effect little,
he could obstruct everything.

During more than a century after the institution
of the Tribuneship, the Commons struggled manfully for the removal of the grievances under which
they laboured ; and, in spite of many checks and
reverses, succeeded in wringing concession after
concession from the stubborn aristocracy.   At length
in the year of the city 378, both parties mustered
their whole strength for their last and most despe-
rate conflict.   The popular and active Tribune,
Caius Licinius, proposed the three memorable laws
which are called by his name, and which were in-
tended to redress the three great evils of which
the Plebeians complained.   He was supported, with
eminent ability and firmness, by his colleague,
Lucius Sextius.   The struggle appears to have
been the fiercest that ever in any community
terminated without an appeal to arms.   If
such a contest had raged in any Greek city, the
streets would have run with blood.   But, even in

the paroxysms of faction, the Roman retained his gravity, his respect for law, and his tenderness for the lives of his fellow-citizens. Year after year Licinius and Sextius were re-elected Tribunes. Year after year, if the narrative which has come down. to. us is to be trusted, they continued to exert, to the full extent, their power of stopping the whole machine of government. No curule magistrates could be chosen; no military muster could be held. We know too little of the state of Rome in those days to be able to conjecture how, during that long anarchy, the peace was kept, and ordinary justice administered between man and man. The animosity of both parties rose to the greatest height. The excitement, we may well suppose, would have been peculiarly intense at the annual election of Tribunes. On such occasions there can be little doubt that the great families did all that could be done, by threats and caresses, to break the union of the Plebeians. That union, however, proved indissoluble. At length the good cause triumphed. The Licinian laws were carried. Lucius Sextius was the first Plebeian Consul, Caius Licinius the third.

The results of this great change were singularly happy and glorious. Two centuries of prosperity, harmony, and victory followed the reconciliation of the orders. Men who remembered Rome engaged in waging petty wars almost within sight of the Capitol lived to see her the mistress of Italy. While the disabilities of the Plebeians continued, she was scarcely able to maintain her ground against the Volscians and Hernicans. When those disabilities were removed, she rapidly became more than a match for Carthage and Macedon.

During the great Licinian contest the Plebeian poets were, doubtless, not silent. Even in modern times songs have been by no means without influence on public affairs ; and we may therefore infer that, in a society where printing was unknown, and where books were rare, a pathetic or humorous party-ballad must have produced effects such as we can but faintly conceive. It is certain that satirical poems were common at Rome from a very early period. The rustics, who lived at a distance from the seat of government, and took little part in the strife of factions, gave vent to their petty local animosities in coarse Fescennine verse. The lampoons of the city were doubtless of a higher order ; and their sting was early felt by the nobility. For in the Twelve Tables, long before the time of the Licinian laws, a severe punishment was denounced against the citizen who should compose or recite verses reflecting on another.*

* Cicero justly infers from this law that there had been early Latin poets whose works had been lost before his time. 'Quamquam id quidem etiam xii tabulæ declarant, condi jam tum solitum esse carmen, quod ne liceret fieri ad alterius injuriam lege sanxerunt.'—*Tusc.* iv. 2.

Satire is, indeed, the only sort of composition in which the Latin poets, whose works have come down to us, were not mere imitators of foreign models; and it is therefore the only sort of composition in which they have never been rivalled. It was not, like their tragedy, their comedy, their epic and lyric poetry, a hothouse plant which, in return for assiduous and skilful culture, gave only scanty and sickly fruits. It was hardy and full of sap; and in all the various juices which it yielded might be distinguished the flavour of the Ausonian soil. ' Satire,' says Quinctilian, with just pride, ' is all our own.' Satire sprang, in truth, naturally from the constitution of the Roman government and from the spirit of the Roman people; and, though at length subjected to metrical rules derived from Greece, retained to the last an essentially Roman character. Lucilius was the earliest satirist whose works were held in esteem under the Cæsars. But many years before Lucilius was born, Nævius had been flung into a dungeon, and guarded there with circumstances of unusual rigour, on account of the bitter lines in which he had attacked the great Cæcilian family.* The genius and spirit of the Roman satirist survived the liberty of their country, and were not extinguished by the cruel despotism of the Julian and

* Plautus, Miles Gloriosus. Aulus Gellius, iii. 3.

Flavian Emperors. The great poet who told the story of Domitian's turbot, was the legitimate successor of those forgotten minstrels whose songs animated the factions of the infant Republic.

These minstrels, as Niebuhr has remarked, appear to have generally taken the popular side. We can hardly be mistaken in supposing that, at the great crisis of the civil conflict, they employed themselves in versifying all the most powerful and virulent speeches of the Tribunes, and in heaping abuse on the leaders of the aristocracy. Every personal defect, every domestic scandal, every tradition dishonourable to a noble house, would be sought out, brought into notice, and exaggerated. The illustrious head of the aristocratical party, Marcus Furius Camillus, might perhaps be, in some measure, protected by his venerable age and by the memory of his great services to the State. But Appius Claudius Crassus enjoyed no such immunity. He was descended from a long line of ancestors distinguished by their haughty demeanour, and by the inflexibility with which they had withstood all the demands of the Plebeian order. While the political conduct and the deportment of the Claudian nobles drew upon them the fiercest public hatred, they were accused of wanting, if any credit is due to the early history of Rome, a class of qualities which, in the military Commonwealth, is sufficient to cover a multitude of offences. The chiefs of the family appear to have been eloquent, versed in civil business, and learned after the fashion of their age; but in war they were not distinguished by skill or valour. Some of them, as if conscious where their weakness lay, had, when filling the highest magistracies, taken internal administration as their department of public business, and left the military command to their colleagues.* One of them had been intrusted with an army, and had failed ignominiously.† None of them had been honoured with a triumph. None of them had achieved any martial exploit, such as those by which Lucius Quinctius Cincinnatus, Titus Quinctius Capitolinus, Aulus Cornelius Cossus, and, above all, the great Camillus, had extorted the reluctant esteem of the multitude. During the Licinian conflict, Appius Claudius Crassus signalised himself by the ability and severity with which he harangued against the two great agitators. He would naturally, therefore, be the favourite mark of the Plebeian satirists; nor would they have been at a loss to find a point on which he was open to attack.

His grandfather, called, like himself, Appius Claudius, had left a name as much detested as that of Sextus Tarquinius. This elder Appius had been Consul more than seventy years before

* In the years of the city 260, 304, and 330.
† In the year of the city 282.

the introduction of the Licinian laws. By availing himself of a singular crisis in public feeling, he had obtained the consent of the Commons to the abolition of the Tribuneship, and had been the chief of that Council of Ten to which the whole direction of the State had been committed. In a few months his administration had become universally· odious. It had been swept away by an irresistible outbreak of popular fury; and its memory was still held in abhorrence by the whole city. The immediate cause of the downfall of this execrable government was said to have been an attempt made by Appius Claudius upon the chastity of a beautiful young girl of humble birth. The story ran that the Decemvir, unable to succeed by bribes and solicitations, resorted to an outrageous act of tyranny. A vile dependent of the Claudian house laid claim to the damsel as his slave. The cause was brought before the tribunal of Appius. The wicked magistrate, in defiance of the clearest proofs, gave judgment for the claimant. But the girl's father, a brave soldier, saved her from servitude and dishonour by stabbing her to the heart in the sight of the whole Forum. That blow was the signal for a general explosion. Camp and city rose at once; the Ten were pulled down; the Tribuneship was re-established; and Appius escaped the hands of the executioner only by a voluntary death.

It can hardly be doubted that a story so admirably adapted to the purposes both of the poet and of the demagogue would be eagerly seized upon by minstrels burning with hatred against the Patrician order, against the Claudian house, and especially against the grandson and namesake of the infamous Decemvir.

In order that the reader may judge fairly of these fragments of the lay of Virginia, he must imagine himself a Plebeian who has just voted for the re-election of Sextius and Licinius. All the power of the Patricians has been exerted to throw out the two great champions of the Commons. Every Posthumius, Æmilius, and Cornelius has used his influence to the utmost. Debtors have been let out of the workhouses on condition of voting against the men of the people : clients have been posted to hiss and interrupt the favourite candidates : Appius Claudius Crassus has spoken with more than his usual eloquence and asperity : all has been in vain; Licinius and Sextius have a fifth time carried all the tribes : work is suspended : the booths are closed : the Plebeians bear on their shoulders the two champions of liberty through the Forum. Just at this moment it is announced that a popular poet, a zealous adherent of the Tribunes, has made a new song which will cut the Claudian nobles to the heart. The crowd gathers round him, and calls on him to recite it.　He takes his stand on the spot where, according to tradition, Virginia, more than seventy years ago, was seized by the pandar of Appius, and he begins his story.

VIRGINIA.

FRAGMENTS OF A LAY SUNG IN THE FORUM ON THE DAY WHEREON LUCIUS
SEXTIUS SEXTINUS LATERANUS AND CAIUS LICINIUS CALVUS STOLO WERE
ELECTED TRIBUNES OF THE COMMONS THE FIFTH TIME, IN THE YEAR OF THE
CITY CCCLXXXII.

YE good men of the Commons, with loving hearts and true,
Who stand by the bold Tribunes that still have stood by you,
Come, make a circle round me, and mark my tale with care,
A tale of what Rome once hath borne, of what Rome yet may bear.
This is no Grecian fable, of fountains running wine,
Of maids with snaky tresses, or sailors turned to swine.
Here, in this very Forum, under the noonday sun,
In sight of all the people, the bloody deed was done.
Old men still creep among us who saw that fearful day,
Just seventy years and seven ago, when the wicked Ten bare sway.

Of all the wicked Ten still the names are held accursed,
And of all the wicked Ten Appius Claudius was the worst.
He stalked along the Forum like King Tarquin in his pride:
Twelve axes waited on him, six marching on a side;
The townsmen shrank to right and left, and eyed askance with fear
His lowering brow, his curling mouth, which always seemed to
        sneer:
That brow of hate, that mouth of scorn, marks all the kindred still;
For never was there Claudius yet but wished the Commons ill:

Nor lacks he fit attendance; for close behind his heels,
With outstretched chin and crouching pace, the client Marcus
    steals,
His loins girt up to run with speed, be the errand what it may,
And the smile flickering on his cheek, for aught his lord may say.
Such varlets pimp and jest for hire among the lying Greeks:
Such varlets still are paid to hoot when brave Licinius speaks.
Where'er ye shed the honey, the buzzing flies will crowd;
Where'er ye fling the carrion, the raven's croak is loud;
Where'er down Tiber garbage floats, the greedy pike ye see;
And wheresoe'er such lord is found, such client still will be.

    Just then, as through one cloudless chink in a black stormy sky,
Shines out the dewy morning-star, a fair young girl came by.
With her small tablets in her hand, and her satchel on her arm,
Home she went bounding from the school, nor dreamed of shame
    or harm;
And past those dreaded axes she innocently ran,
With bright, frank brow that had not learned to blush at gaze of
    man;
And up the Sacred Street she turned, and, as she danced along,
She warbled gaily to herself lines of the good old song,
How for a sport the princes came spurring from the camp,
And found Lucrece, combing the fleece, under the midnight lamp.
The maiden sang as sings the lark, when up he darts his flight,
From his nest in the green April corn, to meet the morning light;
And Appius heard her sweet young voice, and saw her sweet
    young face,
And loved her with the accursed love of his accursed race,
And all along the Forum, and up the Sacred Street,
His vulture eye pursued the trip of those small glancing feet.
    *   *   *   *   *   *   *

Over the Alban mountains the light of morning broke;
From all the roofs of the Seven Hills curled the thin wreaths of
    smoke:
The city-gates were opened; the Forum all alive,
With buyers and with sellers was humming like a hive:
Blithely on brass and timber the craftsman's stroke was ringing,
And blithely o'er her panniers the market-girl was singing,
And blithely young Virginia came smiling from her home:
Ah! woe for young Virginia, the sweetest maid in Rome!
With her small tablets in her hand, and her satchel on her arm,
Forth she went bounding to the school, nor dreamed of shame
    or harm.
She crossed the Forum shining with stalls in alleys gay,
And just had reached the very spot whereon I stand this day,
When up the varlet Marcus came; not such as when erewhile
He crouched behind his patron's heels with the true client smile:
He came with lowering forehead, swollen features, and clenched
        fist,
And strode across Virginia's path, and caught her by the wrist.
Hard strove the frighted maiden, and screamed with look aghast;
And at her scream from right and left the folk came running fast;
The money-changer Crispus, with his thin silver hairs,
And Hanno from the stately booth glittering with Punic wares,
And the strong smith Muræna, grasping a half-forged brand,
And Volero the flesher, his cleaver in his hand.
All came in wrath and wonder; for all knew that fair child;
And, as she passed them twice a day, all kissed their hands and
        smiled;
And the strong smith Muræna gave Marcus such a blow,
The caitiff reeled three paces back, and let the maiden go.
Yet glared he fiercely round him, and growled in harsh, fell tone,
'She's mine, and I will have her: I seek but for mine own:

She is my slave, born in my house, and stolen away and sold,
The year of the sore sickness, ere she was twelve hours old.
'Twas in the sad September, the month of wail and fright,
Two augurs were borne forth that morn; the Consul died ere
    night.
I wait on Appius Claudius, I waited on his sire :
Let him who works the client wrong beware the patron's ire ! '

  So spake the varlet Marcus ; and dread and silence came
On all the people at the sound of the great Claudian name.
For then there was no Tribune to speak the word of might,
Which makes the rich man tremble, and guards the poor man's
    right.
There was no brave Licinius, no honest Sextius then;
But all the city, in great fear, obeyed the wicked Ten.
Yet ere the varlet Marcus again might seize the maid,
Who clung tight to Muræna's skirt, and sobbed, and shrieked for
    aid,
Forth through the throng of gazers the young Icilius pressed,
And stamped his foot, and rent his gown, and smote upon his breast,
And sprang upon that column, by many a minstrel sung,
Whereon three mouldering helmets, three rusting swords, are
    hung.
And beckoned to the people, and in bold voice and clear
Poured thick and fast the burning words which tyrants quake to
    hear.

  ' Now, by your children's cradles, now by your fathers' graves,
Be men to-day, Quirites, or be for ever slaves !
For this did Servius give us laws ?   For this did Lucrece bleed ?
For this was the great vengeance wrought on Tarquin's evil seed ?
For this did those false sons make red the axes of their sire ?
For this did Scævola's right hand hiss in the Tuscan fire ?

Shall the vile fox-earth awe the race that stormed the lion's den?
Shall we, who could not brook one lord, crouch to the wicked Ten?
Oh for that ancient spirit which curbed the Senate's will!
Oh for the tents which in old time whitened the Sacred Hill!
In those brave days our fathers stood firmly side by side;
They faced the Marcian fury; they tamed the Fabian pride:
They drove the fiercest Quinctius an outcast forth from Rome;
They sent the haughtiest Claudius with shivered fasces home.
But what their care bequeathed us our madness flung away:
All the ripe fruit of threescore years was blighted in a day.
Exult, ye proud Patricians! The hard-fought fight is o'er.
We strove for honours—'twas in vain: for freedom—'tis no more.
No crier to the polling summons the eager throng;
No tribune breathes the word of might that guards the weak
     from wrong.
Our very hearts, that were so high, sink down beneath your will.
Riches, and lands, and power, and state—ye have them:—keep
     them still.
Still keep the holy fillets; still keep the purple gown,
The axes, and the curule chair, the car, and laurel crown:
Still press us for your cohorts, and, when the fight is done,
Still fill your garners from the soil which our good swords have
     won.
Still, like a spreading ulcer, which leech-craft may not cure,
Let your foul usance eat away the substance of the poor.
Still let your haggard debtors bear all their fathers bore;
Still let your dens of torment be noisome as of yore;
No fire when Tiber freezes; no air in dog-star heat;
And store of rods for free-born backs, and holes for free-born
     feet.
Heap heavier still the fetters; bar closer still the grate;
Patient as sheep we yield us up unto your cruel hate.

But, by the Shades beneath us, and by the Gods above,
Add not unto your cruel hate your yet more cruel love!
Have ye not graceful ladies, whose spotless lineage springs
From Consuls, and High Pontiffs, and ancient Alban kings?
Ladies, who deign not on our paths to set their tender feet,
Who from their cars look down with scorn upon the wondering
   street,
Who in Corinthian mirrors their own proud smiles behold,
And breathe of Capuan odours, and shine with Spanish gold?
Then leave the poor Plebeian his single tie to life—
The sweet, sweet love of daughter, of sister, and of wife,
The gentle speech, the balm for all that his vexed soul endures,
The kiss, in which he half forgets even such a yoke as yours.
Still let the maiden's beauty swell the father's breast with pride;
Still let the bridegroom's arms infold an unpolluted bride.
Spare us the inexpiable wrong, the unutterable shame,
That turns the coward's heart to steel, the sluggard's blood to flame,
Lest, when our latest hope is fled, ye taste of our despair,
And learn by proof, in some wild hour, how much the wretched
   dare.'

 *   *   *   *   *   *   *
 *   *   *   *   *   *   *

 Straightway Virginius led the maid a little space aside,
To where the reeking shambles stood, piled up with horn and hide,
Close to yon low dark archway, where, in a crimson flood,
Leaps down to the great sewer the gurgling stream of blood.
Hard by, a flesher on a block had laid his whittle down;
Virginius caught the whittle up, and hid it in his gown.
And then his eyes grew very dim, and his throat began to swell,
And in a hoarse, changed voice he spake, 'Farewell, sweet
   child! Farewell!
Oh! how I loved my darling! Though stern I sometimes be,
To thee, thou know'st I was not so. Who could be so to thee?

And how my darling loved me! How glad she was to hear
My footstep on the threshold when I came back last year!
And how she danced with pleasure to see my civic crown,
And took my sword, and hung it up, and brought me forth my
        gown!
Now, all those things are over—yes, all thy pretty ways,
Thy needlework, thy prattle, thy snatches of old lays;
And none will grieve when I go forth, or smile when I return,
Or watch beside the old man's bed, or weep upon his urn.
The house that was the happiest within the Roman walls,
The house that envied not the wealth of Capua's marble halls,
Now, for the brightness of thy smile, must have eternal gloom,
And for the music of thy voice, the silence of the tomb.
The time is come. See how he points his eager hand this way!
See how his eyes gloat on thy grief, like a kite's upon the prey!
With all his wit, he little deems, that, spurned, betrayed, bereft,
Thy father hath in his despair one fearful refuge left.
He little deems that in this hand I clutch what still can save
Thy gentle youth from taunts and blows, the portion of the slave;
Yea, and from nameless evil, that passeth taunt and blow—
Foul outrage which thou knowest not, which thou shalt never
        know.
Then clasp me round the neck once more, and give me one more
        kiss;
And now, mine own dear little girl, there is no way but this.'
With that he lifted high the steel, and smote her in the side,
And in her blood she sank to earth, and with one sob she died.

    Then, for a little moment, all people held their breath;
·And through the crowded Forum was stillness as of death;
And in another moment brake forth from one and all
A cry as if the Volscians were coming o'er the wall.

I

Some with averted faces shrieking fled home amain;
Some ran to call a leech; and some ran to lift the slain:
Some felt her lips and little wrist, if life might there be found;
And some tore up their garments fast, and strove to stanch the
    wound.
In vain they ran, and felt, and stanched; for never truer blow
That good right arm had dealt in fight against a Volscian foe.

When Appius Claudius saw that deed, he shuddered and sank
    down,
And hid his face some little space with the corner of his gown,
Till, with white lips and bloodshot eyes, Virginius tottered nigh,
And stood before the judgment-seat, and held the knife on high.
'Oh! dwellers in the nether gloom, avengers of the slain,
By this dear blood I cry to you, do right between us twain;
And even as Appius Claudius hath dealt by me and mine,
Deal you by Appius Claudius and all the Claudian line!'
So spake the slayer of his child, and turned, and went his way;
But first he cast one haggard glance to where the body lay,
And writhed, and groaned a fearful groan, and then, with stead-
    fast feet,
Strode right across the market-place unto the Sacred Street.

Then up sprang Appius Claudius: 'Stop him; alive or dead!
Ten thousand pounds of copper to the man who brings his head.'
He looked upon his clients; but none would work his will.
He looked upon his lictors; but they trembled, and stood still.
And, as Virginius through the press his way in silence cleft,
Ever the mighty multitude fell back to right and left.
And he hath passed in safety unto his woeful home,
And there ta'en horse to tell the camp what deeds are done in
    Rome.

By this the flood of people was swollen from every side,
And streets and porches round were filled with that o'erflowing
    tide;
And close around the body gathered a little train
Of them that were the nearest and dearest to the slain.
They brought a bier, and hung it with many a cypress crown,
And gently they uplifted her, and gently laid her down.
The face of Appius Claudius wore the Claudian scowl and sneer,
And in the Claudian note he cried, ' What doth this rabble here ?
Have they no crafts to mind at home, that hitherward they stray ?
Ho ! lictors, clear the market-place, and fetch the corpse away ! '
The voice of grief and fury till then had not been loud ;
But a deep sullen murmur wandered among the crowd,
Like the moaning noise that goes before the whirlwind on the
    deep,
Or the growl of a fierce watch-dog but half-aroused from sleep.
But when the lictors at that word, tall yeomen all and strong,
Each with his axe and sheaf of twigs, went down into the throng,
Those old men say, who saw that day of sorrow and of sin,
That in the Roman Forum was never such a din.
The wailing, hooting, cursing, the howls of grief and hate,
Were heard beyond the Pincian Hill, beyond the Latin Gate.
But close around the body, where stood the little train
Of them that were the nearest and dearest to the slain,
No cries were there, but teeth set fast, low whispers and black
    frowns,
And breaking up of benches, and girding up of gowns.
'Twas well the lictors might not pierce to where the maiden lay,
Else surely had they been all twelve torn limb from limb that day.
Right glad they were to struggle back, blood streaming from
    their heads,
With axes all in splinters, and raiment all in shreds.

Then Appius Claudius gnawed his lip, and the blood left his cheek;
And thrice he beckoned with his hand, and thrice he strove to
    speak;
And thrice the tossing Forum set up a frightful yell;
' See, see, thou dog! what thou hast done; and hide thy shame
    in hell!
Thou that wouldst make our maidens slaves must first make
    slaves of men.
Tribunes! Hurrah for Tribunes! Down with the wicked Ten!'
And straightway, thick as hailstones, came whizzing through
    the air
Pebbles, and bricks, and potsherds, all round the curule chair:
And upon Appius Claudius great fear and trembling came;
For never was a Claudius yet brave against aught but shame.
Though the great houses love us not, we own, to do them right,
That the great houses, all save one, have borne them well in fight.
Still Caius of Corioli, his triumphs and his wrongs,
His vengeance and his mercy, live in our camp-fire songs.
Beneath the yoke of Furius oft have Gaul and Tuscan bowed;
And Rome may bear the pride of him of whom herself is proud.
But evermore a Claudius shrinks from a stricken field,
And changes colour like a maid at sight of sword and shield.
The Claudian triumphs all were won within the city towers;
The Claudian yoke was never pressed on any necks but ours.
A Cossus, like a wild cat, springs ever at the face;
A Fabius rushes like a boar against the shouting chase;
But the vile Claudian litter, raging with currish spite,
Still yelps and snaps at those who run, still runs from those who
    smite.
So now 'twas seen of Appius.   When stones began to fly,
He shook, and crouched, and wrung his hands, and smote upon
    his thigh.

'Kind clients, honest lictors, stand by me in this fray !
Must I be torn in pieces ? Home, home, the nearest way ! '
While yet he spake, and looked around with a bewildered stare,
Four sturdy lictors put their necks beneath the curule chair ;
And fourscore clients on the left, and fourscore on the right,
Arrayed themselves with swords and staves, and loins girt up for
    fight.
But, though without or staff or sword, so furious was the throng,
That scarce the train with might and main could bring their lord
    along.
Twelve times the crowd made at him ; five times they seized his
    gown ;
Small chance was his to rise again, if once they got him down :
And sharper came the pelting ; and evermore the yell—
'Tribunes ! we will have Tribunes !'—rose with a louder swell :
And the chair tossed as tosses a bark with tattered sail
When raves the Adriatic beneath an eastern gale,
When the Calabrian sea-marks are lost in clouds of spume,
And the great Thunder-Cape has donned his veil of inky gloom.
One stone hit Appius in the mouth, and one beneath the ear ;
And ere he reached Mount Palatine, he swooned with pain and fear.
His cursed head, that he was wont to hold so high with pride,
Now, like a drunken man's, hung down, and swayed from side to
    side ;
And when his stout retainers had brought him to his door,
His face and neck were all one cake of filth and clotted gore.
As Appius Claudius was that day, so may his grandson be !
God send Rome one such other sight, and send me there to see !

    *   *   *   *   *   *   *

THE PROPHECY OF CAPYS.

THE PROPHECY OF CAPYS.

It can hardly be necessary to remind any reader that according to the popular tradition, Romulus, after he had slain his grand-uncle Amulius, and restored his grandfather Numitor, determined to quit Alba, the hereditary domain of the Sylvian princes, and to found a new city. The Gods, it was added, vouchsafed the clearest signs of the favour with which they regarded the enterprise, and of the high destinies reserved for the young colony.

This event was likely to be a favourite theme of the old Latin minstrels. They would naturally attribute the project of Romulus to some divine intimation of the power and prosperity which it was decreed that his city should attain. They would probably introduce seers foretelling the victories of unborn Consuls and Dictators, and the last great victory would generally occupy the most conspicuous place in the prediction. There is nothing strange in the supposition that the poet who was employed to celebrate the first great triumph of the Romans over the Greeks might throw his song of exultation into this form.

The occasion was one likely to excite the
strongest feelings of national pride. A great
outrage had been followed by a great retribution.
Seven years before this time, Lucius Posthumius
Megellus, who sprang from one of the noblest
houses of Rome, and had been thrice Consul, was
sent ambassador to Tarentum, with charge to de-
mand reparation for grievous injuries. The Tarentines gave him audience in their theatre, where he
addressed them in such Greek as he could command, which, we may well believe, was not exactly
such as Cineas would have spoken. An exquisite
sense of the ridiculous belonged to the Greek
character; and closely connected with this faculty
was a strong propensity to flippancy and imper-
tinence. When Posthumius placed an accent
wrong, his hearers burst into a laugh. When he
remonstrated, they hooted him, and called him
barbarian; and at length hissed him off the stage
as if he had been a bad actor. As the grave
Roman retired, a buffoon who, from his constant
drunkenness, was nicknamed the Pint-pot, came
up with gestures of the grossest indecency, and
bespattered the senatorial gown with filth. Posthumius turned round to the multitude, and held
up the gown, as if appealing to the universal law
of nations. The sight only increased the insolence
of the Tarentines. They clapped their hands, and
set up a shout of laughter which shook the theatre.

'Men of Tarentum,' said Posthumius, 'it will take not a little blood to wash this gown.'*

Rome, in consequence of this insult, declared war against the Tarentines. The Tarentines sought for allies beyond the Ionian Sea. Pyrrhus, king of Epirus, came to their help with a large army; and, for the first time, the two great nations of antiquity were fairly matched against each other.

The fame of Greece in arms, as well as in arts, was then at the height. Half a century earlier, the career of Alexander had excited the admiration and terror of all nations from the Ganges to the Pillars of Hercules. Royal houses, founded by Macedonian captains, still reigned at Antioch and Alexandria. That barbarian warriors, led by barbarian chiefs, should win a pitched battle against Greek valour guided by Greek science, seemed as incredible as it would now seem that the Burmese or the Siamese should, in the open plain, put to flight an equal number of the best English troops. The Tarentines were convinced that their countrymen were irresistible in war; and this conviction had emboldened them to treat with the grossest indignity one whom they regarded as the representative of an inferior race. Of the Greek generals then living, Pyrrhus was indisputably the first. Among the troops who were trained in the Greek discipline, his Epirotes ranked high. His

* Dion. Hal. De Legationibus.

expedition to Italy was a turning-point in the history of the world. He found there a people who, far inferior to the Athenians and Corinthians in the fine arts, in the speculative sciences, and in all the refinements of life, were the best soldiers on the face of the earth. Their arms, their gradations of rank, their order of battle, their method of intrenchment, were all of Latian origin, and had all been gradually brought near to perfection, not by the study of foreign models, but by the genius and experience of many generations of great native commanders. The first words which broke from the king, when his practised eye had surveyed the Roman encampment, were full of meaning:—'These barbarians,' he said, 'have nothing barbarous in their military arrangements.' He was at first victorious; for his own talents were superior to those of the captains who were opposed to him; and the Romans were not prepared for the onset of the elephants of the East, which were then for the first time seen in Italy—moving mountains, with long snakes for hands.* But the victories of the Epirotes were fiercely disputed, dearly purchased, and altogether unprofitable. At length, Manius Curius Dentatus, who had in his first Consulship won two triumphs, was again placed at the head of the Roman Commonwealth,

---

* *Anguimanus* is the old Latin epithet for an elephant. Lucretius, ii. 538, v. 1302.

and sent to encounter the invaders. A great battle
was fought near Beneventum. Pyrrhus was completely defeated. He repassed the sea; and the
world learned, with amazement, that a people had
been discovered, who, in fair fighting, were superior
to the best troops that had been drilled on the
system of Parmenio and Antigonus.

The conquerors had a good right to exult in their
success; for their glory was all their own. They
had not learned from their enemy how to conquer
him. It was with their own national arms, and
in their own national battle-array, that they had
overcome weapons and tactics long believed to be
invincible. The pilum and the broadsword had
vanquished the Macedonian spear. The legion had
broken the Macedonian phalanx. Even the elephants, when the surprise produced by their first
appearance was over, could cause no disorder in
the steady yet flexible battalions of Rome.

It is said by Florus, and may easily be believed,
that the triumph far surpassed in magnificence any
that Rome had previously seen. The only spoils
which Papirius Cursor and Fabius Maximus could
exhibit were flocks and herds, waggons of rude
structure, and heaps of spears and helmets. But
now, for the first time, the riches of Asia and the
arts of Greece adorned a Roman pageant. Plate,
fine stuffs, costly furniture, rare animals, exquisite
paintings and sculptures, formed part of the pro-

cession. At the banquet would be assembled a
crowd of warriors and statesmen, among whom
Manius Curius Dentatus would take the highest
room. Caius Fabricius Luscinus, then, after two
Consulships and two triumphs, Censor of the
Commonwealth, would doubtless occupy a place of
honour at the board. In situations less conspicuous probably lay some of those who were, a
few years later, the terror of Carthage; Caius
Duilius, the founder of the maritime greatness of
his country; Marcus Atilius Regulus, who owed
to defeat a renown far higher than that which he
had derived from his victories; and Caius Lutatius
Catulus, who, while suffering from a grievous
wound, fought the great battle of the Ægates, and
brought the first Punic war to a triumphant close.
It is impossible to recount the names of these
eminent citizens, without reflecting that they were
all, without exception, Plebeians, and would, but
for the ever-memorable struggle maintained by
Caius Licinius and Lucius Sextius, have been
doomed to hide in obscurity, or to waste in civil
broils, the capacity and energy which prevailed
against Pyrrhus and Hamilcar.

On such a day we may suppose that the patriotic
enthusiasm of a Latin poet would vent itself in
reiterated shouts of *Io triumphe,* such as were
uttered by Horace on a far less exciting occasion,
and in boasts resembling those which Virgil put

into the mouth of Anchises. The superiority of some foreign nations, and especially of the Greeks, in the lazy arts of peace, would be admitted with disdainful candour; but pre-eminence in all the qualities which fit a people to subdue and govern mankind would be claimed for the Romans.

The following lay belongs to the latest age of Latin ballad-poetry. Nævius and Livius Andronicus were probably among the children whose mothers held them up to see the chariot of Curius go by. The minstrel who sang on that day might possibly have lived to read the first hexameters of Ennius, and to see the first comedies of Plautus. His poem, as might be expected, shows a much wider acquaintance with the geography, manners, and productions of remote nations, than would have been found in compositions of the age of Camillus. But he troubles himself little about dates, and having heard travellers talk with admiration of the Colossus of Rhodes, and of the structures and gardens with which the Macedonian kings of Syria had embellished their residence on the banks of the Orontes, he has never thought of inquiring whether these things existed in the age of Romulus.

THE PROPHECY OF CAPYS.

A LAY, SUNG AT THE BANQUET IN THE CAPITOL, ON THE DAY
WHEREON MANIUS CURIUS DENTATUS, A SECOND TIME CONSUL,
TRIUMPHED OVER KING PYRRHUS AND THE TARENTINES, IN
THE YEAR OF THE CITY CCCCLXXIX.

I.

Now slain is King Amulius,
  Of the great Sylvian line,
Who reigned in Alba Longa,
  On the throne of Aventine.
Slain is the Pontiff Camers,
  Who spake the words of doom:
'The children to the Tiber;
  The mother to the tomb.'

II.

In Alba's lake no fisher
  His net to-day is flinging:
On the dark rind of Alba's oaks
  To-day no axe is ringing:
The yoke hangs o'er the manger:
  The scythe lies in the hay:
Through all the Alban villages
  No work is done to-day.

K

III.

And every Alban burgher
　　Hath donned his whitest gown :
And every head in Alba
　　Weareth a poplar crown ;
And every Alban door-post
　　With boughs and flowers is gay ;
For to-day the dead are living ;
　　The lost are found to-day.

IV.

They were doomed by a bloody king :
　　They were doomed by a lying priest :
They were cast on the raging flood :
　　They were tracked by the raging beast :
Raging beast and raging flood
　　Alike have spared the prey ;
And to-day the dead are living :
　　The lost are found to-day.

V.

The troubled river knew them,
　　And smoothed his yellow foam,
And gently rocked the cradle
　　That bore the fate of Rome.
The ravening she-wolf knew them,
　　And licked them o'er and o'er,
And gave them of her own fierce milk,
　　Rich with raw flesh and gore.

Twenty winters, twenty springs,
   Since then have rolled away;
And to-day the dead are living:
   The lost are found to-day.

VI.

Blithe it was to see the twins,
   Right goodly youths and tall,
Marching from Alba Longa
   To their old grandsire's hall.
Along their path fresh garlands
   Are hung from tree to tree:
Before them stride the pipers,
   Piping a note of glee.

VII.

On the right goes Romulus,
   With arms to the elbows red,
And in his hand a broadsword,
   And on the blade a head—
A head in an iron helmet,
   With horse-hair hanging down,
A shaggy head, a swarthy head,
   Fixed in a ghastly frown—
The head of King Amulius
   Of the great Sylvian line,
Who reigned in Alba Longa,
   On the throne of Aventine.

VIII.

On the left side goes Remus,
　With wrists and fingers red,
And in his hand a boar-spear,
　And on the point a head—
A wrinkled head and aged,
　With silver beard and hair,
And holy fillets round it,
　Such as the pontiffs wear—
The head of ancient Camers,
　Who spake the words of doom:
'The children to the Tiber;
　The mother to the tomb.'

IX.

Two and two behind the twins
　Their trusty comrades go,
Four and forty valiant men,
　With club, and axe, and bow.
On each side every hamlet
　Pours forth its joyous crowd,
Shouting lads and baying dogs
　And children laughing loud,
And old men weeping fondly
　As Rhea's boys go by,
And maids who shriek to see the heads,
　Yet, shrieking, press more nigh.

X.

So they marched along the lake ;
　　They marched by fold and stall,
By corn-field and by vineyard,
　　Unto the old man's hall.

XI.

In the hall-gate sate Capys,
　　Capys, the sightless seer ;
From head to foot he trembled
　　As Romulus drew near.
And up stood stiff his thin white hair,
　　And his blind eyes flashed fire :
' Hail ! foster child of the wonderous nurse !
　　Hail ! son of the wonderous sire !

XII.

' But thou—what dost thou here
　　In the old man's peaceful hall ?
What doth the eagle in the coop,
　　The bison in the stall ?
Our corn fills many a garner;
　　Our vines clasp many a tree ;
Our flocks are white on many a hill ;
　　But these are not for thee.

XIII.

' For thee no treasure ripens
　　In the Tartessian mine :

For thee no ship brings precious bales
   Across the Libyan brine:
Thou shalt not drink from amber;
   Thou shalt not rest on down;
Arabia shall not steep thy locks,
   Nor Sidon tinge thy gown.

XIV.

' Leave gold and myrrh and jewels,
   Rich table and soft bed,
To them who of man's seed are born,
   Whom woman's milk have fed.
Thou wast not made for lucre,
   For pleasure, nor for rest;
Thou, that art sprung from the War-god's loins,
   And hast tugged at the she-wolf's breast.

XV.

' From sunrise unto sunset
   All earth shall hear thy fame:
A glorious city thou shalt build,
   And name it by thy name:
And there, unquenched through ages,
   Like Vesta's sacred fire,
Shall live the spirit of thy nurse,
   The spirit of thy sire.

XVI.

' The ox toils through the furrow,
   Obedient to the goad;

The patient ass, up flinty paths,
　Plods with his weary load :
With whine and bound the spaniel
　His master's whistle hears ;
And the sheep yields her patiently
　To the loud clashing shears.

XVII.

' But thy nurse will hear no master ;
　Thy nurse will bear no load ;
And woe to them that shear her,
　And woe to them that goad !
When all the pack, loud baying,
　Her bloody lair surrounds,
She dies in silence, biting hard,
　Amidst the dying hounds.

XVIII.

' Pomona loves the orchard ;
　And Liber loves the vine ;
And Pales loves the straw-built shed
　Warm with the breath of kine ;
And Venus loves the whispers
　Of plighted youth and maid,
In April's ivory moonlight
　Beneath the chestnut shade.

XIX.

' But thy father loves the clashing
　Of broadsword and of shield :
He loves to drink the steam that reeks
　From the fresh battle-field :

He smiles a smile more dreadful
  Than his own dreadful frown,
When he sees the thick black cloud of smoke
  Go up from the conquered town.

XX.

' And such as is the War-god,
  The author of thy line,
And such as she who suckled thee,
  Even such be thou and thine.
Leave to the soft Campanian
  His baths and his perfumes ;
Leave to the sordid race of Tyre
  Their dyeing-vats and looms :
Leave to the sons of Carthage
  The rudder and the oar :
Leave to the Greek his marble Nymphs
  And scrolls of wordy lore.

XXI.

' Thine, Roman, is the pilum :
  Roman, the sword is thine,
The even trench, the bristling mound,
  The legion's ordered line ;
And thine the wheels of triumph,
  Which with their laurelled train
Move slowly up the shouting streets
  To Jove's eternal fane.

XXII.

' Beneath thy yoke the Volscian
    Shall vail his lofty brow :
Soft Capua's curled revellers
    Before thy chairs shall bow :
The Lucumoes of Arnus
    Shall quake thy rods to see ;
And the proud Samnite's heart of steel
    Shall yield to only thee.

XXIII.

' The Gaul shall come against thee
    From the land of snow and night :
Thou shalt give his fair-haired armies
    To the raven and the kite.

XXIV.

' The Greek shall come against thee,
    The conqueror of the East.
Beside him stalks to battle
    The huge earth-shaking beast,
The beast on whom the castle
    With all its guards doth stand,
The beast who hath between his eyes
    The serpent for a hand.
First march 'the bold Epirotes,
    Wedged close with shield and spear ;
And the ranks of false Tarentum
    Are glittering in the rear.

XXV.

'The ranks of false Tarentum
  Like hunted sheep shall fly:
In vain the bold Epirotes
  Shall round their standards die:
And Apennine's grey vultures
  Shall have a noble feast
On the fat and the eyes
  Of the huge earth-shaking beast.

XXVI.

'Hurrah! for the good weapons
  That keep the War-god's land.
Hurrah! for Rome's stout pilum
  In a stout Roman hand.
Hurrah! for Rome's short broadsword,
  That through the thick array
Of levelled spears and serried shields
  Hews deep its gory way.

XXVII.

'Hurrah! for the great triumph
  That stretches many a mile.
Hurrah! for the wan captives
  That pass in endless file.
Ho! bold Epirotes, whither
  Hath the Red King ta'en flight?
Ho! dogs of false Tarentum,
  Is not the gown washed white?

XXVIII.

'Hurrah! for the great triumph
　That stretches many a mile.
Hurrah! for the rich dye of Tyre,
　And the fine web of Nile,
The helmets gay with plumage
　Torn from the pheasant's wings,
The belts set thick with starry gems
　That shone on Indian kings,
The urns of massy silver,
　The goblets rough with gold,
The many-coloured tablets bright
　With loves and wars of old,
The stone that breathes and struggles,
　The brass that seems to speak ;—
Such cunning they who dwell on high
　Have given unto the Greek.

XXIX.

Hurrah! for Manius Curius,
　The bravest son of Rome,
Thrice in utmost need sent forth,
　Thrice drawn in triumph home.
Weave, weave, for Manius Curius
　The third embroidered gown :
Make ready the third lofty car,
　And twine the third green crown ;
And yoke the steeds of Rosea
　With necks like a bended bow,
And deck the bull, Mevania's bull,
　The bull as white as snow.

XXX.

'Blest and thrice blest the Roman
  Who sees Rome's brightest day,
Who sees that long victorious pomp
  Wind down the Sacred Way,
And through the bellowing Forum,
  And round the Suppliant's Grove,
Up to the everlasting gates
  Of Capitolian Jove.

XXXI.

'Then where, o'er two bright havens,
  The towers of Corinth frown;
Where the gigantic King of Day
  On his own Rhodes looks down;
Where soft Orontes murmurs
  Beneath the laurel shades;
Where Nile reflects the endless length
  Of dark-red colonnades;
Where in the still deep water,
  Sheltered from waves and blasts,
Bristles the dusky forest
  Of Byrsa's thousand masts;
Where fur-clad hunters wander
  Amidst the northern ice;
Where through the sand of morning-land
  The camel bears the spice;
Where Atlas flings his shadow
  Far o'er the western foam,
Shall be great fear on all who hear
  The mighty name of Rome.'

IVRY:

A SONG OF THE HUGUENOTS.

IVRY.

Now glory to the Lord of Hosts, from whom all glories are!
And glory to our Sovereign Liege, King Henry of Navarre!
Now let there be the merry sound of music and of dance,
Through thy corn-fields green, and sunny vines, oh pleasant land
    of France!
And thou, Rochelle, our own Rochelle, proud city of the waters,
Again let rapture light the eyes of all thy mourning daughters.
As thou wert constant in our ills, be joyous in our joy,
For cold, and stiff, and still are they who wrought thy walls annoy.
Hurrah! Hurrah! a single field hath turned the chance of war,
Hurrah! Hurrah! for Ivry, and Henry of Navarre.

Oh! how our hearts were beating, when, at the dawn of day,
We saw the army of the League drawn out in long array;
With all its priest-led citizens, and all its rebel peers,
And Appenzel's stout infantry, and Egmont's Flemish spears.
There rode the brood of false Lorraine, the curses of our land;
And dark Mayenne was in the midst, a truncheon in his hand:
And, as we looked on them, we thought of Seine's empurpled flood,
And good Coligni's hoary hair all dabbled with his blood;
And we cried unto the living God, who rules the fate of war,
To fight for His own holy name, and Henry of Navarre.

The King is come to marshal us, in all his armour drest,
And he has bound a snow-white plume upon his gallant crest.

He looked upon his people, and a tear was in his eye;
He looked upon the traitors, and his glance was stern and high.
Right graciously he smiled on us, as rolled from wing to wing,
Down all our line, a deafening shout, 'God save our Lord the
　　　King!'
'And if my standard-bearer fall, as fall full well he may,
'For never saw I promise yet of such a bloody fray,
'Press where ye see my white plume shine, amidst the ranks of
　　　war,
'And be your oriflamme to-day the helmet of Navarre.'

Hurrah! the foes are moving.　Hark to the mingled din
Of fife, and steed, and trump, and drum, and roaring culverin.
The fiery Duke is pricking fast across Saint André's plain,
With all the hireling chivalry of Guelders and Almayne.
Now by the lips of those ye love, fair gentlemen of France,
Charge for the golden lilies,—upon them with the lance.
A thousand spurs are striking deep, a thousand spears in rest,
A thousand knights are pressing close behind the snow-white
　　　crest;
And in they burst, and on they rushed, while, like a guiding star,
Amidst the thickest carnage blazed the helmet of Navarre.

Now, God be praised, the day is ours.　Mayenne hath turned his
　　　rein.
D'Aumale hath cried for quarter.　The Flemish count is slain.
Their ranks are breaking like thin clouds before a Biscay gale;
The field is heaped with bleeding steeds, and flags, and cloven mail.
And then we thought on vengeance, and, all along our van,
'Remember St. Bartholomew,' was passed from man to man.
But out spake gentle Henry, 'No Frenchman is my foe:
'Down, down with every foreigner, but let your brethren go.'

Oh! was there ever such a knight, in friendship or in war,
As our Sovereign Lord, King Henry, the soldier of Navarre?

Right well fought all the Frenchmen who fought for France to-day·
And many a lordly banner God gave them for a prey
But we of the religion have borne us best in fight ;
And the·good Lord of Rosny has ta'en the cornet white.
Our own true Maximilian the cornet white hath ta'en,
The cornet white with crosses black, the flag of false Lorraine.
Up with it high ; unfurl it wide ; that all the host may know
How God hath humbled the proud house which wrought His
    church such woe.
Then on the ground, while trumpets sound their loudest point of
    war,
Fling the red shreds, a footcloth meet for Henry of Navarre.

Ho! maidens of Vienna ; Ho! matrons of Lucerne ;
Weep, weep, and rend your hair for those who never shall return.
Ho! Philip, send, for charity, thy Mexican pistoles,
That Antwerp monks may sing a mass for thy poor spearmen's
    souls.
Ho! gallant nobles of the League, look that your arms be bright ;
Ho! burghers of Saint Genevieve, keep watch and ward to-night.
For our God hath crushed the tyrant, our God hath raised the
    slave,
And mocked the counsel of the wise, and the valour of the brave.
Then glory to His holy name, from whom all glories are ;
And glory to our Sovereign Lord, King Henry of Navarre.

1824.

THE ARMADA:

A FRAGMENT.

THE ARMADA.

ATTEND, all ye who list to hear our noble England's praise ;
I tell of the thrice famous deeds she wrought in ancient days,
When that great fleet invincible against her bore in vain
The richest spoils of Mexico, the stoutest hearts of Spain.

It was about the lovely close of a warm summer day,
There came a gallant merchant-ship full sail to Plymouth Bay;
Her crew hath seen Castile's black fleet, beyond Aurigny's isle,
At earliest twilight, on the waves lie heaving many a mile.
At sunrise she escaped their van, by God's especial grace ;
And the tall Pinta, till the noon, had held her close in chase.
Forthwith a guard at every gun was placed along the wall ;
The beacon blazed upon the roof of Edgecumbe's lofty hall ;
Many a light fishing-bark put out to pry along the coast,
And with loose rein and bloody spur rode inland many a post.
With his white hair unbonneted, the stout old sheriff comes ;
Behind him march the halberdiers ; before him sound the drums;
His yoemen round the market cross make clear an ample space ;
For there behoves him to set up the standard of Her Grace.
And haughtily the trumpets peal, and gaily dance the bells,
As slow upon the labouring wind the royal blazon swells.
Look how the Lion of the sea lifts up his ancient crown,
And underneath his deadly paw treads the gay lilies down.
So stalked he when he turned to flight, on that famed Picard field,
Bohemia's plume, and Genoa's bow, and Cæsar's eagle shield.

So glared he when at Agincourt in wrath he turned to bay,
And crushed and torn beneath his claws the princely hunters lay.
Ho ! strike the flagstaff deep, Sir Knight: ho ! scatter flowers,
    fair maids:
Ho ! gunners, fire a loud salute: ho ! gallants, draw your blades:
Thou sun, shine on her joyously; ye breezes, waft her wide;
Our glorious SEMPER EADEM, the banner of our pride.

The freshening breeze of eve unfurled that banner's massy fold;
The parting gleam of sunshine kissed that haughty scroll of gold;
Night sank upon the dusky beach, and on the purple sea,
Such night in England ne'er had been, nor e'er again shall be.
From Eddystone to Berwick bounds, from Lynn to Milford Bay,
That time of slumber was as bright and busy as the day;
For swift to east and swift to west the ghastly war-flame spread,
High on St. Michael's Mount it shone: it shone on Beachy
    Head.
Far on the deep the Spaniard saw, along each southern shire,
Cape beyond cape, in endless range, those twinkling points of fire.
The fisher left his skiff to rock on Tamar's glittering waves:
The rugged miners poured to war from Mendip's sunless caves:
O'er Longleat's towers, o'er Cranbourne's oaks, the fiery herald
    flew:
He roused the shepherds of Stonehenge, the rangers of Beaulieu.
Right sharp and quick the bells all night rang out from Bristol
    town,
And ere the day three hundred horse had met on Clifton down;
The sentinel on Whitehall gate looked forth into the night,
And saw o'erhanging Richmond Hill the streak of blood-red light.
Then bugle's note and cannon's roar the deathlike silence broke,
And with one start, and with one cry, the royal city woke.
At once on all her stately gates arose the answering fires;
At once the wild alarum clashed from all her reeling spires:

From all the batteries of the Tower pealed loud the voice of
    fear;
And all the thousand masts of Thames sent back a louder cheer:
And from the furthest wards was heard the rush of hurrying feet,
And the broad streams of pikes and flags rushed down each
    roaring street;
And broader still became the blaze, and louder still the din,
As fast from every village round the horse came spurring in:
And eastward straight from wild Blackheath the warlike errand
    went,
And roused in many an ancient hall the gallant squires of Kent.
Southward from Surrey's pleasant hills flew those bright couriers
    forth;
High on bleak Hampstead's swarthy moor they started for the
    north;
And on, and on, without a pause, untired they bounded still:
All night from tower to tower they sprang; they sprang from
    hill to hill:
Till the proud peak unfurled the flag o'er Darwin's rocky dales,
Till like volcanoes flared to heaven the stormy hills of Wales,
Till twelve fair counties saw the blaze on Malvern's lonely height,
Till streamed in crimson on the wind the Wrekin's crest of light,
Till broad and fierce the star came forth on Ely's stately fane,
And tower and hamlet rose in arms o'er all the boundless plain;
Till Belvoir's lordly terraces the sign to Lincoln sent,
And Lincoln sped the message on o'er the wide vale of Trent;
Till Skiddaw saw the fire that burned on Gaunt's embattled pile,
And the red glare on Skiddaw roused the burghers of Carlisle.

      *   *   *   *

1832.

www.ingramcontent.com/pod-product-compliance
Lightning Source LLC
Chambersburg PA
CBHW020011030726
47500CB00002B/536